THE SURROGATE FOR A BILLIONAIRE THUG 2

GLITZ

The Surrogate For A Billionaire Thug 2

Copyright © 2025 by Author
All rights reserved.
Published in the United States of America.

All rights reserved. No part of this publication may be reproduced, distributed, or transmitted in any form or by any means, including photocopying, recording, or other electronic or mechanical methods, without the prior written permission of the publisher, except in the case of brief quotations embodied in critical reviews and certain other noncommercial uses permitted by copyright law. For permission requests, please contact: www.authortwylat.com.

This is a work of fiction. Names, characters, places, and incidents either are the products of the author's imagination or are used fictitiously. Any resemblance of actual persons, living or dead, businesses, companies, events, or locales is entirely coincidental. The publisher does not have any control and does not assume any responsibility for author or third-party websites or their content.

The unauthorized reproduction or distribution of this copyrighted work is a crime punishable by law. No part of the book may be scanned, uploaded to or downloaded from file sharing sites, or distributed in any other way via the Internet or any other means, electronic, or print, without the publisher's permission. Criminal copyright infringement, including infringement without monetary gain, is investigated by the FBI and is punishable by up to five years in federal prison and a fine of $250,000 (www.fbi.gov/ipr/).

This book is licensed for your personal enjoyment only. Thank you for respecting the author's work.
Published by Twyla T. Presents, LLC.

Created with Vellum

MAILING LIST

TEXT LIST
TEXT TTP TO 866-311-3517 to receive a text message for each of our releases!

ARE YOU ON THE EMAIL LIST?

Click here https://bit.ly/2MO25jK
to join Twyla T. Presents' mailing list and receive new book release alerts, exclusive giveaways, sneak peeks & more via email!

To my readers:

I just want to say thank you so much for reading this series and supporting me! I'm sorry for the wait but I really hope y'all enjoy this finale! I love y'all!!!

1

Stprix was a ball of nerves as he sat outside of the home that Signy had been occupying. For the past two hours, he had been parked down the block watching her home. His phone rang with a call from Fox but he didn't answer. It was seven o'clock at night when he finally convinced himself to get out of the car.

He walked around, looking through the windows but didn't see anything that looked out of the ordinary. He walked around to the front and knocked on the door. He turned his back and a couple minutes later, he heard the locks turn. He turned around and it felt like time stood still as he roamed Signy's body that had gotten even better than the first time she had given birth.

"What you doing here?" She asked, breaking his trance.

"Can we talk?" He asked, and she walked off from the door. He looked around at all the pink and yellow baby things that decorated her home and felt even sicker than he did when he arrived.

"You gave another nigga a daughter, baby girl?" He asked as Signy sat on the couch. She heard the sadness in his tone, and she just stared at him.

"Why does it matter, Stprix? You showed me just how little I meant to you then you kept showing me over and over again."

GLITZ

He sat down beside her and she scooted over causing him to sigh.

"That wasn't my intention. I know I should've left you alone, but I couldn't and I still can't. I need you in my life. Whatever I gotta do just let me know."

"I'm done."

"Why 'cause you got a nigga now?" He frowned.

"No because you don't value or care about me, and I don't want a man like that, Stprix."

There was a knock at the door, and Signy got up and headed for the door with Stprix's eyes glued to her. She opened it, and Marquin stepped inside holding a car seat with a pink blanket on top.

"You straight?" He asked Signy with his eyes trained on Stprix.

"She good, nigga," Stprix answered for her. He wanted smoke with Marquin. Signy wasn't supposed to entertain another man let alone have his baby.

"I'm okay. Thank y'all for keeping her for me. I slept too good without her crybaby ass."

"Anytime, ain't that right my Story? I love you, ma-ma. Call us if you need us." Marquin lifted the blanket off the car seat and kissed her cheek.

Marquin left, and Signy locked the door and took Story out of her carseat. She walked back towards the couch and sat down. After about ten minutes of silence, Signy looked at him.

"You just gon' sit here and stare at us, Stprix?"

"That was your baby daddy?" Stprix asked a question of his own that he was dying to know the answer to.

"Nope," she replied as Story began to cry.

"Can I see her? What's her name?"

"Why?" Signy asked as she pulled her breast out an began to feed her.

"You finna break a nigga heart even more with this shit, Fat."

Signy ignored him while she fed and burped her. Story didn't fall asleep like she normally did after some milk, she was wide awake.

"Story, I really wanted to keep you from him but that's not fair of me." Signy stared into her face before kissing her nose.

2

She passed Story to Stprix and watched as he examined her. She had his skin complexion, the same birthmark on her leg that all his children had, and her hair was full of curls. Tears streamed down his cheeks as he cradled her.

Stprix held her close to his chest while he cried. Signy was so mad at him but in that moment, she scooted close to them and wrapped her arm around his shoulder. He turned and embraced her, careful not to hurt the baby.

"I'm so sorry."

"It's not about us right now." Signy stroked his head as he laid his head on her shoulder. Once he settled, he sat up and stared into Story's face.

"She looks just like Saint. Why you didn't tell me you was pregnant, baby girl?"

"I didn't know. I wasn't showing or sick. I was about to board a plane when my water broke, and my friend and her dude drove me to the hospital."

"That was that nigga?" He asked, and Signy heard the bitterness in his tone.

"Yes." She laughed because he seemed different but she knew the real Stprix was lying dormant and waiting to expose his toxic behavior.

"What's her full name, Signy?"

"Story Rainbow Alexander," Signy revealed.

"When y'all coming back home?" He asked, locking eyes with her.

"I'm not and I'm not about to argue with you about it either, Stprix, so just enjoy your daughter."

"That's not fair, Fat. You know her brothers are going to want to see her, hell they hounding me about you, especially that lil' nigga, Stox," he said, causing her to smile. Stox didn't play about her, and she didn't play about him.

"I love me some Stox. I love all your boys. You can bring them here anytime, but I'm not going back to Nashville, not until she's at least six months. I don't want her being exposed to germs and shit."

He acted like he didn't hear her as he studied the beauty before

GLITZ

him as she stared back at him with her hazel eyes that were identical to his.

"I'm not leaving, then. You think I'ma let the next nigga bond with my daughter before me?" He twisted his face up, and she rolled her eyes.

"Do whatever you want to do, me or nobody else ain't ever stopped you from doing what Stprix wants to do. You not staying here though." Signy walked up the steps, and they were right behind her.

"What's that supposed to mean?"

"Do what you been doing."

"I been sick as hell without you. I damn sholl ain't been thinking about no bitch. I ain't had sex sin-"

"Since you fucked my girlfriend." She scoffed at that.

"I don't give a fuck about that girl, Signy," he said, following her into her room.

"But I did!" She yelled at him, causing Story to whine.

"I was wrong. I know that now."

"Stprix, you knew it then, please don't stand in my face and play with me. I'm not the bitch I used to be, thanks to you."

"I'm sorry, Fat. I should've let you be but I couldn't. I still can't. You and my daughters my whole universe. I ain't tryna move on without you. You been fucking?"

"I haven't been thinking about a nigga or a bitch thanks to you, so no, I haven't. I've been in therapy trying to get back to myself."

"Can I come with you?"

Signy walked in the bathroom and closed the door. Stprix heard the shower turn on. He looked at Story, who was staring at him.

"Hey, Rainbow. Daddy loves you so much. I'm so glad you're here and healthy. Hopefully, you can make your mommy come around for Daddy. I can't wait to make memories with you." Stprix smiled at her with tears in his eyes. Story was their rainbow baby, and Signy had given her the perfect name because she had a story to tell.

She nodded off, and Stprix laid her inside her crib. He kicked his shoes off and a few minutes later, Signy walked out with steam following her. She had a towel wrapped around her body. She walked towards the bassinet and checked on Story. She turned around, and Stprix was behind her. He stared down into her face, making her nervous.

"Move that towel."

"Nigga, what?"

He pulled her towel, leaving her in her birthday suit. His eyes went to her pussy that still had his name tatted across it.

"It's finna get covered up." She pushed him back but he wrapped her in his arms, hugging her tight.

"I'm never giving up on you. I don't care if it's ten years from now. I want to die with you, baby."

"You want me to shoot you in your face, 'cause we can make that happen, right now."

Stprix pecked her lips while she frowned. He continued to kiss her while she stood rigidly still. He gripped her cheeks, and she grabbed his forearms as his tongue slid into her mouth. Their tongues danced for what seemed like forever until Signy pulled away from him. She put her hand up on his chest.

"What's up when we going to therapy?"

"Why do you want to be with me, now? You didn't before." Signy grabbed a gown out of her dresser and pulled it over her head.

"So now you lying. We both said we wasn't ready to settle down. I'm ready, though. I know it's gonna take some time for us to get back to us, but I'm willing to do whatever it takes."

"I don't want to talk about us, Prix. I love you, I always will, but this is about our baby. I'll let you stay, but I've sulked about you for almost a year so we can be fri- nah we can be roommates. You go your way, I go mine. I don't know what the future holds for us, only God does, but right now I just want to enjoy my baby." She walked up on the bassinet, peering down at Story. Stprix walked up behind Signy, cornering her in.

"I love you too, Fat, and thank you so much for both of my daughters. I'll give you space but I'm not going nowhere."

*　*　*

SIGNY WAS IN THE BED, sleeping. Story was in her bassinet beside the bed unbeknownst to her, crying. Stprix got up off the couch in the sitting area of Signy's bedroom and picked Story up. He changed her diaper and fed her before they got on the couch. Stprix laid down with her on his chest and in no time, they were sleeping again.

Signy awoke and looked across her room with a smile on her face. She had witnessed Stprix be a great father but he was different with Rainbow as he called her. Signy went into the bathroom to handle her hygiene. Then, she pulled on a robe and headed for the kitchen. She cooked them breakfast then went outside on the porch with her cup of coffee. Her mouth opened and closed she walked down to the all-white McLaren P1. She opened the door and was greeted with hot pink seats. There was one rainbow-colored rose on the seat and under it was an envelope. She opened it and smiled.

I feel like the last time I did this is 'cause I did some dumb shit. Here we are again 'cause I did some even more fuck shit. I know you tired of hearing me tell you I'm sorry, but I am. I love you, and I appreciate everything about you, Fat. Thank you for my girls and thank you for just being in a nigga life.

P.S. I sent you the money you paid in rent for this house plus some and not because I'm trying to buy my way back into your life but because you deserve it all. Two apiece and one more just 'cause you my whole world, Fat.

P.P.S. Pop the trunk

She flipped the page and the deed to the house she was parked in front of was behind it. They had been together for two weeks, and Signy was glad to have him. He had been the help that she needed. She logged into her account to see he had sent her five million dollars. She hated how much she still loved Stprix. For two weeks, she had been avoiding him at all cost. Even when he took his place on her couch in her room every night, she made sure to already be asleep when it was bedtime.

She got out and opened the trunk and there was a Goyard, Chanel, and five Hermes bags inside. She also a ton of diamond rings and four matching twenty-seven karat tennis necklaces and the matching bracelets. Signy snapped so many pictures. Stprix had big stepped for her and even though they were beefing, she was thankful. He had fit so much into the little push present he gifted her. She walked towards the cobblestone walkway and up the stairs. She smiled at the sight of Stprix standing there rocking Story.

"Good morning, Fat," Stprix greeted as she walked inside.

"Good morning, baby daddy." She kissed Story's cheek.

"Baby daddy? Rainbow you hear that Daddy making progress," Stprix cooed.

Signy rolled her eyes at him then went into the kitchen and washed her hands before making their plates. Then, she took Story and breastfed her while Stprix ate.

"Everything to your liking?"

"Yep," she said dryly, causing him to laugh. "Thank you, ugly, but you're not making progress. I'm going out tonight, remember? You sure y'all gon' be okay?"

Stprix ignored her because she was acting like Story wasn't his ninth child.

"Go 'head on you act like this my first baby. Ain't that right, Daddy Rainbow?"

"You really shouldn't hold her all the time. She's going to be spoiled," Signy fussed.

"I can't help it. It's been weeks, and I'm still shocked we have another daughter."

"You? Hell, tell me about it but I'm glad she's here with her lil' fat self." Signy took her from Stprix. She rubbed her nose against hers, causing Story to smile.

"Who you going out with?" Stprix pried, and Signy tried to read him.

"Why?"

"I'm just curious."

"Curiosity killed the cat."

"I'm trying to kill yours," he said and watched as she squirmed under his gaze.

"Thanks to you, I'm gay again." She rolled her eyes at him. He got

7

GLITZ

up and put his plate in the sink. He kissed Story's forehead before kissing Signy's lips.

"That lil' friend of yours better stop tryna play matchmaker before I show her nigga who the fuck I am." He walked out of the kitchen, and she watched him until he disappeared.

She really didn't plan on having no dealings with Stprix but they had another daughter that was alive and well, and neither of them wanted to leave her for too long.

Signy ate her breakfast then went back upstairs to her room where Stprix was. He was on the couch watching TV. Signy passed him Story before she got back in the bed.

"You finna sleep all day?"

"Maybe, what's it to you? You want the room across the hall since you ain't leaving?"

"Nah. I told you I ain't going nowhere."

2

Signy was in the club feeling herself. She had on a white Chrome Heart white beater that she wore as a dress with a black thong underneath. On her feet were a pair of chrome boots. She had on all her new ice, and she was looking like a light show. After her nap earlier, she went and got a full set, a pedicure, and got her hair done. It was styled in long bundles that hung past her ass.

"Let me find out you over there fucking on that nigga, Ms. McLaren pussy." Jocelyn walked in their section along with Marquin.

"Stay out my business, bitch! What's up, Quin?" Signy spoke to them while her and Joycelyn embraced.

Marquin walked off and a few minutes later, three bottle girls approached their section with bottles. They began their turn up right away. Marquin came back with his brother in tow. Signy was supposed to get to know him on their trip but Story had made her grand entrance to the world.

"Sis, this my big brother, Lynx. Lynx this Signy. I been trying to introduce y'all forever," Marquin said while Lynx took in Signy's beauty. Her dress was painted on her voluptuous body.

"Perfect timing. What's up, beautiful, it's nice to finally meet you." Lynx took her hand in his and kissed the back of it.

GLITZ

"Likewise." Signy blushed until she thought about Stprix's threat. If he would murder his own family, she knew nobody was safe from him.

Jocelyn pulled Signy up on the couch with her, and they danced for three songs until their feet were hurting. Lynx sat beside Signy, tossing his arm over her shoulder.

"You gon' keep running from a nigga or can I finally get some of your time?" He whispered in her ear and goosebumps formed on her skin.

"I'm not dating right now," she admitted, truthfully. For one, Stprix was lurking and it was no telling what he might do.

"I ain't tryna hear that shit. Let a nigga take you to get something to eat when we leave." He picked up her hand and intertwined their fingers.

"Okay," Signy reluctantly agreed. She pulled out her phone, texting Stprix, letting him know she no longer needed a ride home.

They stayed for an hour then left walking out the front doors. Signy and Jocelyn shared glances before focusing their attention on Stprix, who was leaned up against his truck.

"I'll be back," Signy said to Lynx. She walked down the steps to Stprix. He put his arms around her waist, pulling her body against his. His hands went to her ass cheeks.

"I thought I told you I had a ride." Signy cocked her head to the side.

"Yeah, nah that ain't gon' work for me. Let's go, Fat, before I lose my patience."

"Can I go tell my friend bye?" Signy asked, and he released her.

Signy walked towards them and gave Jocelyn a hug.

"I'll call you tomorrow. Get my number from her if you still want it. Bye, brother," Signy said to all three of them. She walked back towards Stprix, and he opened the door and she climbed in.

She looked in the backseat to find Story sleeping. Stprix got in and pulled off. The ride back to her house was done in silence. Signy unlocked the door, and they followed her in. She walked upstairs to her bedroom and was blown away.

"This crazy muthafucka." There was now a king-sized bed in her sitting area that was perfectly made up like it belonged there.

She couldn't believe him but then again, she could because it was Stprix. She walked in her closet and undressed. Then, she went into the bathroom to handle her hygiene. She got dressed in a gown and put her bonnet on. She walked into her bedroom, and Stprix and Story were in her bed. Signy walked out the room and headed for the kitchen. She poured her a shot and tossed it back. Then, she looked through the refrigerator. She made lasagna, salad, and garlic bread before she went out. She made another plate then sat down and ate before washing her hands and heading back upstairs.

Stprix had Story on his chest while he scrolled on his phone. Signy walked towards the bed and picked her up. Stprix's hand went to her ass, trapping her on side of his bed. His hand went under her gown, and he rubbed her ass cheeks in slow circles.

"You was about to leave with that nigga?"

"He asked me to get something to eat. I was coming home to my baby."

"You wasn't coming home to me, Fat?" Stprix locked eyes with her as he slid a finger inside of her, causing her to gasp. For a minute, she lost her train of thought as they stared at one another. She hated how she was like putty in his hands.

"I'm her-e-e," she stumbled over her words as he inserted another finger inside her walls that were squeezing his fingers.

"Put her in her bed," Stprix demanded. Signy didn't want to because Story was the only thing keeping Stprix off her. She nervously shook her head as he smirked.

"You ain't gotta put her down, Fat, but I'ma beat yo' ass if you drop my baby." Stprix entered another finger, and her mouth dropped open. She placed Story in her bassinet that was beside his bed.

He pulled her in the bed and pulled her gown over her head. He took her in from head to toe. He pressed his lips into hers while spreading her legs. They kissed until their tongues were wrestling with each other. He slid two fingers in her, and she spread her legs even wider. He licked her nipples slowly then bit them before sucking them into his mouth. He kissed his way down her body and twirled his tongue in her belly button. He pulled his coated fingers from her middle and placed them in his mouth. Gripping her ankles he lustfully stared in between her legs.

"Fat, I missed you." Stprix buried his face into her wet center. He nibbled on her clit, sucked it into his mouth, and shook his head back and forth.

"Fuckkkk! I hate youuu," Signy moaned lowly but he heard her.

His tongue entered her while he stroked her clit hastily until she was cumming in his mouth. He put her foot into his mouth and sucked her toes while their eyes were fixated on each other.

"Prix?"

"What, Fat?"

"Put it in," she demanded as he flipped her over onto her knees. He pushed her back in and buried his face in between her thighs again. He assaulted both holes until she had cum twice more.

Signy helplessly stared at him as he got out of the bed and walked in the bathroom. A few minutes later, he walked out with a warm rag and wiped in between her legs. He peeped at Story, who was still sleeping. He went back into the bathroom and came out, and Signy barely had her eyes open. Stprix got in the bed and pulled her body close to him. They went to sleep in each other's embrace.

Story's cries awoke Stprix a few hours later and he got up and fed and changed her before getting in the bed with her on his chest and Signy at his side. He felt whole with them. He was the happiest he had ever been and it didn't matter that Signy was giving him her ass to kiss because he was just happy to be breathing the same air as her.

* * *

SIGNY WAS SEATED on the couch across from her therapist. Signy hadn't seen her since she had given birth and had informed her about everything that had went on in her life.

"So, how is it co-parenting with Stprix?" Krystal asked.

"It's honestly been fine. He refuses to leave my house but I don't mind because he's very helpful with me and Story. A small part of me missed him. I'm not mean to him but I'm not nice either."

"Why is that?"

"You know why. What do you mean." Signy nervously laughed.

"But Signy, I get you being angry with him for what he did, but how long are you going to keep this up?"

"I don't know until I feel better, I guess." Signy shrugged.

"Let me ask you this, do you see a future without Stprix in it?"

Signy avoided Krystal's unwavering gaze. She knew the answer without having to think about it.

"No. I'm just still trying to get over what he did to me."

"That's understandable. When you're ready to forgive him, do it for you and not what your parents and friends will think about you. They don't have to live your life, only you do. Why don't you bring him to one of your sessions?"

Signy nervously laughed at that because little did Krystal know, he had been asking to attend.

"He's actually been asking to come, so I'll do that the next time." Signy looked down at the time on her Rolex and realized their time was coming to an end.

"Well, that's our time. Call me if you need anything and think about what it is that you want out of life. I look forward to seeing you and Stprix when you return." Krystal stood, then Signy stood, and they shook hands.

Signy left with a lot of thoughts running through her head. A month had passed since Stprix picked her up from the club and although they had a great night, they were still distant. He still occupied his bed in her room. They were in a weird space. Story was two months and a good baby but she was spoiled thanks to Stprix.

Her phone rang with a call from Stprix as if he heard her thoughts. She answered for him as she merged onto the intestate.

"We about to go. You sure you don't want to come?"

"No I'll be waiting for y'all when y'all come back."

"You gon' be waiting for me too, Fat?" Stprix questioned, and she heard the smile in his voice.

GLITZ

"Yes, baby daddy. You got me spoiled too. So don't stay gon' too long."

"Therapy must've been real good, huh? Hurry up and get here." He ended the call, and she turned the radio up.

Twenty minutes later, she pulled up to the clear port and hopped out of her car. She walked towards the jet and boarded the stairs. She found Stprix and Story. She was in her car seat kicking her legs like crazy while laughing.

"Hey, Momma's girl!" Signy unhooked her from her car seat and kissed all over her face, causing Story to laugh.

"How long y'all gon' be gone?"

"I told you like two weeks. Jaquie is here. If you need something just call me. The rules still the same."

"Rules?" She frowned because she knew he was getting at some bullshit.

"No ni—"

"Stprix, you don't have that luxury anymore. We barely cordial and you're giving out demands." She took her eyes off Story to glare at him.

"I ain't tryna upset you. Especially after everything you've been through 'cause of me. But I'm telling you right now or maybe I shouldn't tell you but if you fuck another nigga, I'm going to kill him, so do whatever you want to do, baby girl." Stprix walked off, leaving her with her thoughts and Story. And just like that, he had pissed her off again, even though she wasn't thinking about another man at all.

"I hope you have fun, baby. I love you so much. I hope I don't miss you too much 'cause trust I'll get on the first thing smoking to get to you," Signy cooed while Story stared back at her with a smile like she knew what she was saying.

Stprix appeared, watching Signy strap her back into her car seat. She walked past him, and he reached out and grabbed her, pulling her into him.

"I'm sorry." He kissed the back of her neck.

"No you're not," she argued with a hint of laughter in her tone.

He turned her to face him, wrapping his arms around her waist.

"I am sorry for what I did, Fat. I shouldn't have did it. I want you to know that it had nothing to do with you but everything to do with me being a selfish nigga. It didn't mean shit. It ain't a woman walking that can make me feel the way you do. I'm all in about you. I want to marry you and spend the rest of my life with you if you'll let me."

Signy's eyes watered because even though he'd hurt her, she still loved him very much. Some nights, she awoke in the middle of the night and just stared at him.

"So you're coming to therapy with me when y'all get back?"

"Whatever it takes," he promised.

"Okay, no bitches," she tossed out a demand of her own.

"It's been a year. I ain't thinking about no pussy unless it's the fat one that got my name on it." He gripped her pussy through her velour pants, causing her clit to jump.

"You promise? And if that's true, why you didn't give me none that night?" She challenged, referring to the night he picked her up from the club. That was the only intimate moment they shared since he'd been there.

"On my daughters, Fat. I don't deserve to have you in that way. I'm working my way back or at least I'm trying," he said desperately.

"You are, and I appreciate you being patient with me."

"You got it. Be good. I love you."

"I love you too," she responded for the first time in a long time.

Stprix pressed his forehead into hers, and they stood like that for the longest time until Signy pulled away. She went and gave Story a kiss to the lips then Stprix walked her to her car.

3

Signy was at the club with Jocelyn. She had been kid free for a week and didn't know what to do with herself. She missed Story and Stprix's overbearing presence.

"What you over there, thinking about that nigga?"

"I was thinking about my lil' family. I actually miss them," Signy said with a smile, causing Jocelyn to suck her teeth and roll her eyes.

"Girl, marry that nigga already."

"No thanks. I'm good." Signy looked across the room at the baddie that she had been stealing glances at all night. The woman looked up that time, holding Signy's unwavering gaze.

. . .

"THAT NIGGA HAD you so deep in your feelings, I forgot pussy was your first love. She is bad though but what if she ain't gay?" Jocelyn asked as the bottle girls approached the woman's section that was occupied by her and two other women.

"That ain't got shit to do with me. I'm just trying to make her mine for the night." Signy held her glass up as one of the bottle girls pointed her way.

"And that nigga is cool with your shenanigans?"

Signy ignored her before making her way across the club after realizing the woman was making a move for the bathrooms. Signy took a spot outside and patiently waited for her to come out. She was shocked to see Signy standing there.

"What's up, Sexy?" Signy flirted.

"Hey, why you sending me bottles and shit, you gon make my nigga think a nigga sent them."

"Why you think I sent them?" Signy looked her up and down in appreciation. She hadn't been with a woman since her and Charlene, and she was ready to change that.

"I don't know but I'm not gay. I appreciate the gesture. Honestly, I'm flattered. You're beautiful," the woman said, and Signy smirked.

"Thank you, next time." Signy turned to walk away when the woman grabbed her hand.

"Wait, come have a drink with me. After all, you bought it."

"What's your name?"

"Star. What's yours?"

"Signy." Signy followed her to her section, and she introduced Signy to her friends.

Signy took two shots with her while her friends stood around dancing in their own worlds.

"It was nice meeting you, Star. I gotta get back to my friend."

"Is that a *friend* friend or like a girlfriend?" Star pried.

"She's my best friend. She has a nigga and so do I, truthfully, I just thought you were beautiful and wanted to end my night with you." Signy shrugged as if it wasn't nothing.

"Doing what?" Star asked.

"Come find out." Signy unlocked her phone and passed it to her.

"Tell that nigga you staying with your friends, and I'll come get you," Signy demanded, as she watched her type her number in her phone. Star called her own phone in case she decided to take Signy up on her offer.

"Bye, Signy!" Star called out as Signy walked off. Jocelyn rolled her eyes at her when she finally joined her again.

"What the fuck wrong with you?"

"Bitch you just left me not even for a nigga but a whole bitch. I'm ready to go. You get on my nerves!" Jocelyn got up, stomping out of their section.

Signy followed behind her until they were inside of the back of the truck Marquin sent for them.

"I'm sorry. I wasn't trying to be gone that long." Signy picked up her hand. Jocelyn tried to snatch away from her. Signy kissed the back of her hand, causing Jocelyn to cut her eyes at her.

"Ew stop! Gay bitch!" Jocelyn snapped, causing Signy to laugh. She tried to pull her hand back again but Signy wasn't budging.

Signy's phone went off with a text message. She unlocked it and smiled at the message from Star. Star had sent her the looking eye emoji, and Signy sent it back before locking her phone. They were almost to Signy's home. Signy scooted close to Jocelyn, wrapping her arms around her waist and laying her head on her shoulder.

"You jelly, Jos?"

"Girlll, you fucking wish," Jocelyn argued, and they laughed.

They pulled up in front of Signy's home, and Signy opened the door. Her phone began ringing with a call from Star.

"Hello?" Signy answered, stepping out and putting the phone up against her chest.

"Call me tomorrow, Jos, with yo mean ass. I love you."

"Fuck you, hoe. I love you more," Jocelyn said before Signy closed the door.

Signy headed to her car and got behind the wheel.

* * *

SIGNY AND STAR got on the elevator hand in hand. Signy led her to their suite for the night, and they walked inside. Signy pulled the bottle from her bag and sat it on the nightstand.

Star jumped as her phone rang with a call from her boyfriend, causing Signy to laugh.

"I'm staying at Stephanie's until you get back home," she said while Signy opened the bottle and turned it up. "Okay I love you too," Star said as she watched Signy head for the stairs.

Signy walked into the bathroom and secured her hair before undressing down to her birthday suit. She got in the shower and began washing up. The door to the shower opened, and Signy watched in admiration as Star stepped inside.

"Does this make me gay?" Star asked.

"It makes you whatever you want to be. Don't nobody but me and you got to know about this if that'll make you feel better." Signy walked towards her because she was standing on the opposite end of the shower like she was frozen in fear.

"I can't believe I'm here." Star laughed nervously.

"Do you want to be here?" Signy asked as she washed her body.

"Yeah I do," she admitted causing Signy to smirk. They washed up and got out, then went into the room.

Signy dropped her towel, and Star's eyes roamed her body.

"Did that hurt?" Star asked, referring to her tattoo.

"Hell yeah it hurt." Signy twisted her face up, causing her to laugh. They got in the bed, and Star became even more nervous.

Signy's phone rang with a FaceTime from Stprix. Stox's handsome face filled the screen when she answered instead of Stprix, causing Signy to smile.

"Heyy, son! I miss you. What your sister doing?"

"She with Pops. She just woke up crying but now she back sleeping. We watching scary movies, look." Stox turned the camera around to see Stprix had all his kids in his room.

"Give me my phone, nigga," Stprix said, causing Signy and Star to laugh.

GLITZ

"What's up, Fat?" Stprix stared at her and saw someone's shoulder against hers while they sat up on the pillows against the headboard.

"Nothing. Y'all good?"

"Yeah don't be doing nothing you ain't got no business doing," he warned.

"I'm not. Let me see my baby, nigga," Signy demanded, and Stprix positioned the camera on Story.

"Aww, I wish I could hug and kiss her. Good night Momma Rainbow," Signy cooed.

"What you doing?"

"What it look like, Stprix. I'm in the bed," she sassed, and he stared at her for a minute.

"Okay. I love you."

"I love you more. Call me when she gets up." Signy hung up and put her phone on the charger.

"That was your boyfriend?" Star pried, causing Signy to laugh.

"Yeah, you can say that, we not together right now though."

"Tell me anything." Star playfully rolled her eyes. She turned the bottle of liquor up, knowing she needed more liquid courage to get her through whatever Signy had in store for her.

"So, what made you decide to give me a chance?" Signy quizzed. Signy took the bottle from her hands and turned it up herself before putting it on the nightstand.

"I was just curious is all." Star shrugged.

"Well, how about we put your curiosity to rest," Signy said, and Star became even more nervous.

"Kiss me," Signy demanded.

They stared into each other's eyes as Star made her move. She pressed her lips into hers, and Signy eased her tongue into her mouth. Star captured her tongue, sucking it while Signy moaned into her mouth. She mounted Signy, and Signy gripped her titties as she stared up at her.

"You want to stop?" Signy asked with her eyes on her bare pussy.

Star leaned forward and pressed her chest against Signy's and kissed her lips. Signy spread her legs slightly and their clits found each other as they began rocking against each other. Signy gripped her meaty ass cheeks and pushed her body further into hers while she spread her legs even wider.

"Ouuu shit! Fuckkkk! I'm finna cummmm!" Star moaned as her body began to tremble against hers. Signy was right behind her, holding her close. They clung to each other, kissing like crazy. Signy flipped her over on her back and dove in face first. That night, she turned Star out and introduced her body to some new pleasure.

4

Signy opened the door, coming face to face with Star. Four days had passed since their night of passion. Signy had taken her on a couple dates, and they had chilled at her house a couple of times. Signy was surprised to see her because she didn't invite her or let her know she was on her way.

"Hey." Star held bags of food in her hands.

"Hey," Signy spoke back while stepping to the side. They had been talking nonstop since that night.

Star walked in, closed the door behind her, and locked it. Signy hoped Star passed the vibe check but only time would tell.

"What you doing here?"

"I wanted to spend the day with you."

"Ohhhh! You must want me to eat that pussy again. You ain't slick," Signy teased, and Star rolled her eyes with a laugh.

"Shut up. It was good though. I never knew sex with a woman could be so…"

"So liberating."

"Yeah." Star nodded as she sat the food down on the table.

Star turned the TV on and pulled their containers out. Signy sat down and her stomach growled, causing Star to frown.

"Shut up. Thank you for feeding me."

"It was my pleasure." Star smirked, and Signy caught the double meaning behind her words.

"I ain't gay," Signy mocked, throwing her words back at her.

"Yes, you are you real gay." Star wagged her tongue at her. Signy just shook her head at her.

"You enjoyed it 'cause you popping up at my crib and shit." Signy smirked.

"I did a little bit too much." Star laughed, causing Signy to laugh.

They ate their food silently for a few minutes. Star looked up from her plate then looked back down at it again.

"I want to do it again." Star locked eyes with Signy while licking her lips. Star sat her container down and straddled Signy's lap while pulling her shirt over her head.

Signy's hands groped her body while Star kissed her. The sudden knocking at the door alarmed them. It was the sound of the knocking that alarmed them; whoever was knocking wasn't leaving until someone opened the door. Star stood, pulling her shirt back on. Her phone began ringing as the knocking continued. Signy grabbed her gun out of the couch and got up. She walked to the door and looked out, seeing a man she didn't recognize. She opened the door, and the man pushed his way inside.

"Excuse you! Can I help you?" Signy snapped as he headed towards Star.

"What are you doing here? I told you I was having girls day with my friend. Signy this is my boyfriend, Mitch. Mitch, this is Signy," Star introduced the two.

Jaquie stepped inside, gaining everyone's attention.

"You good?" He asked Signy while staring at the intruder or at least that's how Jaquie viewed him.

"Yes. I'll let you know if I need you," Signy assured him.

He walked out but not before giving the man another look.

"My bad. I did pull up on good bullshit. Y'all enjoy y'all's day. It was nice to meet you, Signy." Mitch stuck his hand out.

"It's cool. My baby daddy the same way, maybe even worse. It was

GLITZ

nice to meet you too." Signy shook his hand. Then, he hugged Star while kissing her lips. She walked him out and a couple minutes later, she walked back in.

"Damnnnn. He ruined the mood didn't he?"

"Kind of." Signy laughed with a shrug.

"Who was that man?"

"My baby daddy's friend. He's here for emergency purposes only."

"What if we get caught?"

"No, bitch! What if *you* get caught? My nigga don't care if I mess with women."

"Why not?" Star frowned her face up in confusion because cheating was cheating to her anyway.

"He's the first and only man I have ever been with. I guess that nigga turned me bisexual, so he don't trip about women."

"Oh okay. Sorry I'm all in your business."

"It's cool. Now you got me ready to ask this nigga why me being with a woman doesn't bother him." Signy frowned, and Star laughed. "I'm dead ass. That nigga is not playing with a full deck," she said as her phone began ringing with a call from him. She knew it was coming after Mitch's visit.

"What the fuck going on?" Stprix questioned as soon as she answered. She got up and walked upstairs to her bedroom.

"It was a misunderstanding. My friend's dude pulled up thinking she was with a nigga. He was respectful. I'm good, calm down baby daddy." Signy tried reasoning with him.

"Your friend or a bitch you fucking 'cause I know yo' lil' freaky ass." He groaned, causing her to laugh.

"Does it matter?"

"Nah but I asked so tell me what I wanna know."

"We had sex. Why doesn't it bother you when I'm with women but you waterboarded me just for giving a man my number. What's the difference?"

"Fat, stop bringing that shit up. When we locked in locked in, you ain't fucking nobody but me. Have your lil' fun while you can."

"You still didn't answer my question," she whined.

"'Cause man, you fucked me on some you was in your feelings type shit. You think I'ma let you give another nigga my shit? You been gay your whole life I'on give a fuck about that. What I look like telling you can't do something that's second nature to you? I know your little history but ain't nobody had you the way I got you. You mine," he said, and she smacked her lips in annoyance.

"Cocky muthafucka. I was in my feelings but that's what I wanted," she argued.

"I know. You was begging for the dick," he teased.

"Shut up! Where my baby at?"

"She in there with Katelyn and Fox. I was just calling to check on you. I love you, Fat," he said, and she couldn't help but to smile. She had been mean to Stprix for the longest and if anything, she felt that his love for her had quadrupled.

"I love you, kiss Rainbow for me."

"Gladly with yo' pussy eating ass." He hung up in her face and she burst out laughing. She couldn't stand Stprix but she loved him so much, more than she had ever loved anyone. He was right; no one had her like he did.

"Signy! Where are you?" Star shouted while walking around, looking for her.

Signy left her bedroom and closed the door behind her. She walked out, coming face to face with Star.

"Do I need to leave?"

"Nah, you good unless you scared."

"Scared of what?"

"Me? That nigga?" Signy gripped her hips, pulling her close. Star rolled her eyes, with a giggle.

"Girl, anyways. Can you fuck me like you did the other night, please?" She pressed her lips against Signy's, and they found themselves kissing until they were on the floor of the hallway, pulling each other's clothes off.

* * *

GLITZ

Signy sat on the couch alongside Stprix while they sat across from Krystal.

"Hello, Stprix, it's nice to finally meet you. I've heard a lot about you." Krystal gave him a warm smile, and he nervously ran his hand over his waves.

"Likewise, even though I'm nervous." It wasn't much he was scared of but he was scared of losing Signy.

"You don't want to be here?" Krystal asked, looking up from her tablet.

"I'm here because she asked me to be, and I'm willing to do whatever it takes to get us on the right path," he answered truthfully.

"Can I ask you this? Where you two ever on the right path?" Krystal asked Stprix, who looked at Signy.

"What you mean?"

"You know what she means." Signy mugged him, and he stroked his beard.

"I wouldn't say that. She was doing her, and I was doing me."

Krystal tapped away at her iPad, before focusing her attention on the couple.

"Signy, you agree?" Krystal asked, and she nodded. "So how did we get here if you two were never on the right path to begin with?"

Signy and Stprix turned, looking at each other.

"Even though we were doing our own thing, we were involved like we were in a relationship."

"And you both ended up hurt, am I correct?" She asked.

"Yes," they said in unison. Signy turned her attention on Stprix, glaring at him.

"So I didn't get hurt too, Fat? You busted my car up and you know what else you did." Stprix turned, facing her.

"You're a billionaire, and that hurt you? 'Cause you and Charlene *both* hurt me, especially you because I expected more from you after everything we've been through together. I don't think you understand how you made me feel in all of that. Like do you even care?" Signy's eyes misted, and she refused to shed any tears. She wiped her eyes before continuing.

"The reason I feel like you don't care is because you pursued her in my father's club, knowing him or anybody could have seen you. I walked in the club and spotted y'all all over each other. Then, I went upstairs for a better view. You say you know how wrong it is now, but you knew it was wrong before you did it. I asked you where you were and you said home. Then, you called me and confessed your love to me while you was doing me dirty. That's not love. I don't want that kind of love."

Signy experienced two heartbreaks in one. She was devastated that they both cheated on her with each other, but Stprix hurt her the most because she was in love with him.

"You're right. I was dead ass wrong. I knew it then, and I know it now. You didn't deserve that."

"So, why did you do it?" Signy asked. It was their first official time to hash out their problems.

"It ain't no reason why. I was still kind of in my feelings about you giving my cousin your number and the aftermath of that situation but even still, I was wrong."

Signy stood, walking out. She needed a break. She paced the hallway, and the door opened. She expected to see Stprix but instead it was Krystal.

"I just need a minute. I'll be back in," Signy assured her.

"You sure? We can always finish another day." Krystal gently grabbed her arm to stop her from aimlessly walking back and forth.

"No. I'm ready to get this over with."

Krystal nodded her head then went back inside, leaving Signy to her thoughts. Five minutes later, she walked back in and sat down on the couch.

"What made you get up and leave?" Krystal quizzed.

"He didn't want me to give my number to any man. Well, I did. The man ended up being his cousin and a whole bunch of drama started because of it. I didn't know it was his cousin, and he was mad because he felt like I shouldn't have given the man my phone number to begin with. He got even, though." Signy couldn't even look at him anymore.

She was starting to think bringing Stprix to her therapy session was a bad idea.

"Stprix, if you don't mind me asking why didn't you want to fully commit to her but wanted her loyalty?"

"I'm committed to her. I've been committed to her whether we put a label on what we were doing or not. The things I do for her and the way I treat her, I don't do for or treat nobody like that. I want to be with her when we get past th—"

"If we get through this," Signy corrected.

"Aight, Signy. Fuck it. Why you even tell me to come to this shit if this is how you was gon' act?" Stprix was defeated. He didn't know what else he could do to get her to forgive him but he was desperate. One minute, she was cool and the next minute, she was hotter than fish grease.

"I'll see you later, Krystal. Thank you!" Signy walked out in a haste. She got in her McLaren and peeled off.

5

Signy and Jocelyn walked into the strip club hand in hand. Signy couldn't believe she had come back to Nashville but she felt bad for not visiting Saint's resting place. Katrina had been holding her down in her absence, and she was thankful.

Signy reserved them a section, and they were instantly seated. After all, it was her father's place of business. A few minutes later, Saad walked up with two of Signy's cousins.

"Oh my God! Felix and Sutton!" Signy jumped up, and they took turns hugging her.

"Not my lil' baby a grown woman now. Who is this?" Felix looked Jocelyn up and down.

"This is my best friend, Jocelyn. Jos, these are my cousins, Felix and Sutton."

Saad hugged Signy, rocking from side to side. He missed his one and only child. Signy was grateful that their relationship had changed for the better. He had been a great father and grandfather.

"I'm about to go see my girls. Your cousins will be with you all night. Call me if you need me." Saad kissed her forehead as bottles were brought to their section.

GLITZ

"Daddy. you didn't have to send all that, it's just us. Kiss my baby for me and tell Momma I'll be to get her tomorrow."

"Yo momma already told you she's not giving you our baby back until you leave, now bye. I love you."

"Anyways. I love you, too," Signy said as he walked off. She turned up with her peoples. Almost two hours later, they were drunk and having the time of their lives.

"Look, twin, she bad!" Jocelyn put her arm around Signy's shoulder, pointing towards the dancer that was twirling around the pole. Signy had never seen her before. Even though she had been gone for a year, she recognized all the other familiar faces.

"Real bad. Come on!" Signy pulled Jocelyn up and they, along with Sutton and Felix, walked out onto the stage from their section.

I Luv Her by Glorilla and T-Pain was blasting from the speakers as Signy tossed money in the air. Signy was mesmerized as she flipped upside down in front of her.

"Welcome home, Signyyyyy!" The DJ announced, and Signy smirked. It had been a minute since she was home and it felt good to be back in her city.

"Fuck you smiling for? Bitch, you got a home in Charlotte with me don't get no ideas," Jocelyn warned, pointing her finger in her face.

"Calm down, Deanna, be cool," Signy said, and they bust out laughing.

"Walk me to the bathroom, please," Signy begged. Jocelyn grabbed her hand, and they walked off the stage.

They walked in the bathroom and relieved their bladder. After washing their hands and making sure their makeup was still flawless, they walked out.

"Signy!" Someone called out, gaining Signy and Jocelyn's attention.

Signy turned around and got a whole attitude at the sight of Charlene.

"Who is that?" Jocelyn asked, sensing the change in Signy's demeanor. They hadn't known each other long but their relationship was solid, and they were truly thankful for each other.

"Nobody." Signy turned around and walked off.

Charlene walked in front of them, cutting off their path as the dancer that was just on stage walked up.

"Hey, baby when did you get here?" She greeted Charlene, who was focused on Signy.

"It looks like you got your hands full." Signy turned her nose up at Charlene.

Signy and Jocelyn walked back to the section and continued their turn up.

"That must've been her. We could've beat her ass if that's what you wanted to do. Matter of fact!" Jocelyn stood, and Signy pulled her back down.

"I'm good, best. Fuck her," Signy promised as Charlene walked up, causing Signy to sigh.

"I know you don't got nothing to say to me but I really need to talk to you. Please," Charlene pleaded while Jocelyn pulled her earrings off.

"Come on. I'll be back y'all," Signy said to Charlene, Jocelyn, and her cousins. The only reason she agreed was because Jocelyn was eager to get her hands on her.

Signy led her outside to her car. They got in, and Signy stared straight ahead, waiting for Charlene to talk.

"I'm sorry. I never meant to hurt you—"

"Please don't play in my face," Signy warned.

"I didn't. We was lit as fuck. Stprix wasn't even trying to take it there with me, but I convinced him it was okay since we had already slept together. I really didn't mean to hurt you. I still love you, Signy," Charlene admitted.

"Did Stprix put you up to this shit?"

"What! No! I haven't seen or talked to him since that night. That was a mistake. I regret it so much." She sighed.

"I regret a lot of shit too," Signy admitted, and Charlene faced her.

"I should've stopped fucking with you when he beat your baby daddy ass and damn sure shouldn't have called you over my house to have a threesome. Y'all both did me dirty but I'm good. You feel better

GLITZ

now?" Charlene didn't miss the sarcasm that was oozing from her tone.

"You really hate me now?" Charlene asked somberly.

"I wouldn't say hate but I don't fuck with you. I'm surprised you didn't find another club to dance at," Signy said as she watched Stprix pull into the parking lot.

"I thought about it but honestly, I was hoping I would run into you one day. I told your daddy a couple of times to let you know I asked about you. He didn't tell you?"

Signy rolled her eyes before laughing. Saad had never played about her. When she was growing up he just needed to be around more, and he would've won an award for best dad ever.

"He didn't tell me nothing," Signy continued to laugh, thinking about Saad. Their relationship had really changed for the better.

"Okay, Signy, well it was good seeing you. You look good. Congratulations on your baby, she's beautiful."

"Thank you and I always look good." Signy watched Stprix walk into the club.

She opened her door, letting Charlene know their conversation was over. Charlene got out, and Signy walked off. Charlene walked up behind her, wrapping her arms around her waist and Signy felt absolutely nothing.

"I miss you. Please forgive me, Si. Please unblock me," Charlene whispered in her ear before kissing her neck. Signy stopped in her tracks. She was slightly discombobulated after that kiss.

"Don't you have a girlfriend?" Signy pulled away from her and faced her. Signy could read the room. She knew the baddie was involved with Charlene.

"She's not you."

"Nobody is. I want to fuck." Signy smirked, and Charlene's eyes lit up.

"Come on."

"No. I want to fuck your bitch so it'll make me feel better." Signy watched Charlene's face drop and felt instant satisfaction. Then she walked into the club and found Jocelyn and her cousins.

She spotted Stprix at the bar with a woman in his face. They hadn't really been talking since therapy but they were in contact. They had to be, they shared a living child together. Signy watched him for three minutes, then she got up and Jocelyn was right behind her.

"What the fuck you doing? And why the fuck you in here any-damn-way." Signy sandwiched herself in between him and the woman that was standing too close to Stprix in her opinion. Stprix hadn't been to Saad's since she caught him and that she was sure Saad would tell her.

He wrapped his arms around her waist and looked down into her face with a big smile on his face. He kissed her lips, and she wanted to snap her head back but they had an audience.

"You know why I'm here. You here. Aria this my wife, Signy. Signy, this my god sister, Aria." Stprix introduced them, and Signy wanted to melt right where she stood.

"Hello, beautiful, it's nice to meet you!" Aria spoke and Signy turned in Stprix's arms so that she was standing face to face with Aria.

"You too! This my friend, Jocelyn," Signy said as Jocelyn waved.

Stprix lowered his head to Signy's ear while Jocelyn and Aria busied themselves with conversation. Signy wasn't trying to take it there with Stprix but it was getting harder and harder. Even though a year had passed, they were still in love. Signy was mad at herself a lot of times for still loving him.

Stprix said his goodbyes to Aria then he grabbed Signy's hand, who grabbed Jocelyn.

"I have to go tell my cousins bye." Signy stopped Stprix, who was headed towards the door. They made a quick detour, and Signy hugged her cousins goodbye then they left.

"You getting in the car with me?" Stprix asked, and she nodded.

"You gon' be good or you want us to stay at my house with you?" Signy asked Jocelyn, passing her her keys.

"I'm a big girl. Be careful. I love you."

"I love you too. Call me if you want me to come back." They exchanged hugs then Signy got in with Stprix.

GLITZ

* * *

SIGNY AWOKE the next morning beside Stprix. He had her wrapped in his embrace. She got up, thinking about her life. She never saw a future with a man let along Stprix but he was her future, which was shocking to herself and others around her. However, the only opinion that mattered was hers. She walked in the bathroom, washed her face, and brushed her teeth. She got in the shower, and a couple minutes later, Stprix walked in standing at the sink. He too brushed his teeth and washed his face. He got in the shower with Signy, and she froze up. They hadn't been that close in a long time. Last night was the first time they slept in the same bed in a while.

"What you doing in here, Stprix?" Signy continued to lather her body.

"What it look like?" He frowned his face up, and she just rolled her eyes because it was clear he woke up on the wrong side of the bed.

They silently showered together, and Signy got out first. She wrapped a towel around her body and walked into his bedroom. She got dressed in a tracksuit out of the new wardrobe he had bought for her. The doorbell went off while he was walking in the room with a towel secured around his waist. Signy stepped into her house shoes and made her way downstairs with her phone in hand. She opened the door coming face to face with Monique.

"Where's Stprix?" Monique walked inside. Signy ignored her as she turned and walked into the kitchen. Monique followed her. Signy washed her hands and made a plate from the food the chef had prepared for them.

Monique began making a plate, and Signy sighed in annoyance.

"It's a sink and soap right over there. All you have to do is take a few steps that way, turn on the faucet, wet your hands, and pump some soap in your hands." Signy turned her lip up in disgust.

"Bitch, I'm not stupid or slow. I know how to wash my hands, the fuck!" Monique snapped.

"I can't tell, you just walked in here from outside and the first thing you do is get in the food. Trifling hoe."

Monique laughed loudly, causing Signy to roll her eyes. All the time that passed and neither of them could stand the sight of each other.

"I'm a trifling hoe but you had a threesome with your nigga and girlfriend, and then they fucked behind your back. You and your pussy a joke, bitch." Monique laughed while Signy ate her food.

"If my pussy a joke why you ain't got your baby daddy back? Move on, bitch, you acting like you want to fuck or some shit. You mad because I told you to wash your hands, some shit your mammy or granny should've taught you to do when you walk in someone's house and get in their food but it's clear they didn't have class either, 'cause just look at you, you wack, tacky ass bitch," Signy spazzed as Stprix walked in the kitchen.

"Aye y'all chill out with all that shit. What you doing here, Mo?" Stprix snapped.

"Can we talk in private?" Monique asked, looking Signy up and down.

"Girllllll! I'm about to go see Story, Stprix." Signy tossed her food in the trash, thanks to Monique she didn't have a appetite anymore. She attempted to walk past them but Stprix grabbed her. He kissed her lips, and she stuck her tongue in his mouth just because she knew Monique was watching. Signy pulled away from him, wiping his mouth with her thumb.

"Take my truck, the keys in there. Kiss my baby for me and tell her I'll be over there tomorrow."

"Okay. I'm never coming off yo' baby daddy, hoe." Signy walked off with a smirk on her face.

"I can't stand that bitch," Signy heard Monique say as she walked out. She got in Stprix's Range Rover and headed towards her momma's house. Twenty minutes later, she pulled into her garage and got out.

She beat on the door, and Katrina opened the door holding Story. Signy eagerly took her and kissed all over her face.

"Hey, Momma! Hey, Momma's favorite girl! I missed you so much.

How did she sleep?" Signy asked as Story stared at her with a smile. Signy walked in the house, following Katrina to the living room.

"Granny's girl was a perfect little angel. You're not getting her until you leave girl, so I don't know why you're here," Katrina said in all seriousness.

"I know, Momma. I just missed my baby." Signy stared down into her face while Story stared back.

"Where's my son-in-law?"

"Son-in-law," Signy repeated, and Katrina gave her the look of death.

"Momma, please go head on with that. Is you cool?"

"Signy, you know that you're going to end up with Stprix. Me and your dad have come to terms with that and yo' ass needs to get on board. I'm sick of that nigga calling me crying all the got damn time," Katrina fussed.

"He be calling you all the time?"

"Yes, child, and I told him I wouldn't say anything but I think you should know all the effort that he is putting in to be with you. I know what he did was wrong as hell but if you're not going to be with him tell him that so his worrisome ass can quit calling me." Katrina groaned, causing Signy to laugh.

6

Stprix walked through a house party alongside Fox and Katelyn. The music was so loud he couldn't hear himself think. There were kids dancing around. Weed smoke floated in the air. Katelyn yanked Stprix's arm and pointed in the direction of their sons. Stprix walked towards them, and their eyes got big as saucers. Storm stepped closer to Stox, hoping his big brother could save him. Stprix snatched both of them up, gaining everybody's attention. The music cut off and the lights flickered on.

"Let's go 'fore I embarrass y'all in here." Stprix turned them a loose and walked off. Stox and Storm were right behind him.

They all walked out, and Stprix nodded his head towards his G Wagon. They got inside, leaving Fox, Stprix, and Katelyn alone.

"Don't be too hard on them," Katelyn said to Stprix before walking towards the truck to hug and kiss her sons. They disobeyed her and were about to be punished and now she was feeling bad.

"Fuck she call me for, then?" Stprix mugged Katelyn, causing Fox to laugh.

"Shid she called both of us," Fox added.

"Look, I was doing something. You should've came and dealt with them lil' niggas." Stprix griped.

Fox looked him up and down. He was dressed in sweats a T-shirt and slides like he ran out of the house.

"You look like you was about to be knee-deep in some pussy," Fox cracked.

"Hell nah, I was trying to. Shid, I was real close. I need that." Stprix was pissed and Fox could see it all over him.

"I'll just take 'em with me if you finna do all that extra shit."

"Too late, I'm here now and she wants to see them anyways. I'm gon', nigga." They slapped hands before Stprix walked towards his truck.

He got in and swung on Stox, who was in the passenger seat. Then, he reached in the backseat and hit Storm. He pulled off and the truck was silent for a minute because he was trying to calm himself.

"So, y'all lil niggas think y'all grown?" Stprix asked and neither one of them said a word. Stprix glanced at Stox, who had his fist balled at his sides and laughed.

"You mad, lil' nigga? You think I give a fuck about that shit! I had to get up out my bed at one o'clock in the morning 'cause y'all went to a high school party that y'all momma told y'all, y'all couldn't go to. Ain't neither one of y'all in high school and ain't neither one of y'all grown."

"My bad, Pops. We shouldn't have went but I told my girlfriend I was coming," Storm spoke up from the back seat while Stox stared straight ahead with his arms folded across his chest.

"I don't give a damn. When y'all momma tell y'all not to do something don't fucking do it. End of story. You ain't got shit to say, Stox?"

Stprix watched his face twist up like he was annoyed with the whole conversation.

"Nope," Stox replied as they drove through the steel gates. Stprix pulled in front of his fountain and they got out. They walked up the cobble stone steps, and Stprix unlocked the door.

They walked in, Stprix held his hand out, and Storm put his phone in his hand. Stox walked past him, and Stprix snatched him up, hemming him against the wall.

"Why the fuck you being disrespectful, muthafucka, when you

know you wrong like I won't beat yo' ass!" Stprix raised his voice as Signy walked down the stairs with Story in her arms after hearing them come in.

"Talk!" Stprix demanded.

"My bad, Daddy, but it ain't even that serious. You didn't have to come in there and embarrass us like that. I'm about to be fourteen. My girlfriend was in there and everything."

"I don't give a fuck if the president of the United States of America was in there. If yo momma tell you don't do something, don't do it. I'ma knock yo' ass out the next time you disrespect me. You really playing with me." Stprix placed him on his feet and thumped his forehead. Stox glared at him while he rubbed his forehead.

"Here, both of y'all go call y'all momma and apologize then bring me y'all's phones. Don't turn them TVs on either," Stprix warned while passing Storm his phone. Storm kissed Signy's cheek and Story before running up the stairs.

Stox hugged her before taking Story from her. He kissed her cheeks while he carefully carried her up the stairs.

"Don't be doing him like that, nigga. What's wrong with you?" Signy mushed Stprix.

"That lil' nigga got me fucked up. He was being disrespectful, why you think I snatched him up and not Storm? Can we pick up where we left off?" Stprix pulled her close until their bodies were pressed against each other. He kissed her neck over and over until she lost her train of thought.

"No, your daughter up now." She tried to push him away, but he wasn't budging.

"Come on, Fat. You wasn't even supposed to have her anyways, you went over there and begged to get her."

"Okay, I'm sick of you and my momma. So you saying you don't want my baby here, nigga?" She smacked her lips in anger.

"I'm saying I want some pussy and you tryna use her to not give me some."

Signy jumped up into his arms, and he carried her up the stairs to his bedroom. He dropped her on the bed and headed for the door.

"Where you going?" Signy yelled.

"They taking too long," Stprix said as there was a knock at the door. Stox walked in, holding Story, and Storm was right behind them.

They passed their phones off and then headed for the door.

"She sleep, son?"

"Yes ma'am. I'ma be up for a minute, you can come get her whenever you want to, but I missed her," Stox answered, causing Signy to smile.

"What you gon' be up for, you ain't got a phone and you can't watch TV," Stprix cracked, and Stox mugged him. Stprix hated his attitude at times because he was a carbon copy of himself. Out of all of his kids, Stox mirrored him the most.

"Y'all can have y'all phones for tonight and your TV but if y'all daddy take it back in the morning, I'm not in it." Signy got up and walked upon Stprix and held her hand out. He looked at her like she was crazy but she wasn't backing down. After what she felt like was a pointless stare down, he gave her their phones.

"Thank you, Ma." Stox was the first to speak.

"You're welcome. Don't disobey your parents again, you either, Storm. Y'all not grown."

"Yes ma'am," they said in unison, causing Stprix to chuckle. They rushed out the room, and he locked the door behind them.

"You finna pay for that shit." Stprix picked her up and dropped her on the bed again. He removed her pants and panties. Buttons went flying in the air when he ripped her shirt open.

She sat up and he pushed it off her shoulders. She pulled him into the bed with her, and their lips found each other. Stprix pulled his shirt over his head while she stroked his dick. She eased his sweats down until they both were in their birthday suits. Signy laid on her back while he laid in between her legs. He pressed his lips against her second set of lips.

"We good, Fat?" Stprix looked up at her, and she nodded. "You sure?" He quizzed, while spreading her lips and exposing her pink center. He licked her up and down slowly before sticking his tongue inside her.

"Yesss!" She moaned as he wrapped his lips around her clit.

He intertwined their fingers after they put their palms up against each other's. He gently nibbled and sucked her clit until she was squeezing his fingers and cumming for the first time. He continued his assault for the next eight minutes, and she was cumming again. He didn't stop there and she snatched away from him, trying to push his head away but he grabbed her hands.

"Fuck my mouth, Fat," he grumbled with a mouthful of pussy.

"I can't," she whined as she lazily thrust her hips at him.

He slid a finger inside her, stroking his finger in a come here motion, and her whole body twitched as she squirted everywhere. He licked her clean then came up, hovering over her. He picked up her legs, holding them in his arms and slid into her, causing them to moan in unison.

"Baby daddy, I missed you!" She moaned as he stretched her walls, the deeper he went.

"I missed you too, Fat." He stared at her pussy as his dick slid in and out of her.

He flipped them over so that he was on his back. Signy hopped on her feet and slid down on his dick. She placed her hands up against his and intertwined their fingers while she bounced up and down at a fast pace.

"Shit! Fuckkk!" Stprix bit his bottom lip that was firmly tucked in between his teeth. She spun around and slammed her ass down on his lap. His hands came up, smacking her ass cheeks.

"Slow down, baby." Stprix wasn't trying to cum but he was so close to exploding inside her.

She ignored him as she watched his toes bend and crack. His moans were like music to her ears. She was breaking him down and enjoying every minute of it. He sat up, gripping a handful of her hair. He yanked her head back as he filled her womb with his semen. He kissed all over her back. She twerked on his dick, and it grew again. He flipped her over on her back and sucked her clit into his mouth.

Then, he pinned her legs behind her head and slid into her. He rotated his hips in a circle, stirring her center.

"Play with that pussy, Fat," he demanded, and she put her hand in between them and stroked her flower.

Stprix's dick grew harder as he watched her face contort into pleasure and her eyes roll to the back of her head. She was on the verge of cumming for the fourth time thanks to Stprix ,and she didn't know if she could take anymore. She snatched her hand back.

"What the fuck I say?" Stprix growled as he slammed in and out of her.

"Baby, I can't," she moaned as her back rose off the bed. Her body shook as he pulled out and watched her juices shoot everywhere. He stroked her clit fast while she helplessly cried out as more of her essence rained down on him.

"Stpriiiiiiiiiiiix! Oh my God, I love you soooo much!" She bust out crying. She was experiencing too much pleasure at one time, and her body had overloaded.

"I love you more, baby girl, more than anything." He kissed her tears while he slid back into her.

She gripped his face and kissed him with so much passion. She was at war with herself for wanting to take Stprix back but she wanted him. She needed him. He flipped her over onto her knees, she put an arch in her back, and he spread her ass cheeks. He buried his face inside. He licked and sucked her asshole while she threw her ass back at him. His hand came down, colliding with her skin. He reached around her and stroked her clit. When she started trembling again, he slid into her asshole and she came again for the fifth time. Stprix was the only person in the bedroom that she was scared of. His dick was past toxic. Signy was helpless as he gripped her waist and slammed her down on his dick while they both moaned uncontrollably.

"I'm finna nut, got damn, I love yo' ass girl." He roughly gripped her hair, pulling her head back. He bit her neck before sucking it.

Signy threw her ass back at him at a rapid pace despite him begging her to slow down. He barely pulled out and when he did, his nut erupted everywhere. They both collapsed on the bed, laying side by side. Stprix walked in the bathroom and brushed his teeth before starting the shower. Signy picked up her phone and FaceTimed Stox.

"She's still sleeping. She good, ma." Stox didn't give Signy a chance to say anything.

"Okay, I'll be to get her. Call me if you need me," Signy said, and he hung up, causing her to laugh. She loved how Story's brothers already didn't play about her. She walked in the bathroom and grabbed a rag before joining Stprix. He had soap suds all over his body.

"You didn't want me to get in the shower with you?" She pouted, and he pulled her towards him.

"I want to do everything with you. I want to get in your skin, Fat. A nigga obsessed with you."

"Why you have to ruin our trust?" She asked as she laid her head against his chest.

"I'm sorry." He got down on his knees, wrapping his arms around her waist and laying his head against her stomach. Signy was beyond special to him. She was his world and although he had messed up bad, he was hoping he could keep her.

"I forgive you, Stprix, but you don't get another chance to hurt me." She pulled him up and he scooped her up, sat on the bench, and pressed his lips into hers.

"Thank you, and I'll never hurt your heart again, only this pussy." He cuffed it and it all of a sudden, had a heartbeat of its own.

"It hurt too, but I want you to hurt it some more," she admitted, causing him to smirk.

"We gotta hurry up. I gotta go get my favorite girl before she wakes up looking for me."

"I thought I was your favorite girl." She playfully pouted, and he kissed her lips.

"You are outside of my beautiful ass daughters that look just like yo' fine ass." He wrapped his hand around her ponytail and yanked her head back. She mounted him, and he eased his dick into her dripping center.

7

Signy was at home in Charlotte on the couch under her blanket, watching TV. Story was beside her in her bassinet sound asleep. Signy had her candles lit and a glass of wine in hand. Her phone vibrated in her hand with a text from Star. Signy hadn't been talking to her since her and Stprix made things official. She opened the message and was shocked to learn Star was outside. Signy glanced at Story before getting up. She unlocked the door, and Star was standing on the other side.

"Is it a bad time?"

"It's okay. What you doing here? I told you I was working shit out with my baby daddy." A month had passed since they made up, and it was a beautiful month well spent. They stayed in Nashville for two full weeks and then went to Charlotte.

"I know but I miss you," Star admitted. Signy's phone rang with a call from none other than Stprix; he always had the worst timing. She didn't answer, and he called right back.

"I miss you too, but we can't kick it like we used to," Signy softly let her down.

"You miss her?" Stprix's voice sounded off throughout her house, and they both jumped. Story began to cry. He was nowhere in sight.

"Where are you?" Signy was nervous as ever because she knew Stprix and how his elevator didn't go all the way to the top.

"I'm at home. Walk your company out, my girl, and get my daughter 'fore you really make me mad."

Signy picked Story up, who was crying. Then, she headed for the door behind Star, who had hightailed it to the door. Signy walked her down to her car. Thanks to Stprix she was so embarrassed.

"Girllll, and I thought my nigga was crazy. I guess you can't have fun with girls nomo. I'm sad but at the same time I'm happy for you. Take care of you and baby girl." Star kissed her lips and hopped inside her car.

Signy looked down at Story, who was staring at her. Signy dreaded walking back inside to face the music but if she was outside too long, Stprix was going to assume she was up to no good. Once Star was gone, she walked back in the house and locked the doors.

She picked up her ringing phone off the couch and answered the FaceTime from Stprix.

"So you put cameras up in my house and didn't tell me?"

"Yeah. Why she popping up at your house and you telling her you miss her?"

"I was just being nice. I don't know why she popped up."

"Okay, I'm about to go be nice then," he said, and Signy ended the call. He called back but she refused to answer. His voice filled the room again.

"I'm just playing, baby girl. You know I'm not fucking up my family for nothing and you ain't either. We done with pussy."

"Go to hell, Stprix, and stop spying on me. What is wrong with you?" She laughed as her phone rang with a regular call.

"I told you I was obsessed with you," he said as soon as she picked up.

"You're creepy. Come take these cameras down. You know damn well I'm not gon' cheat on you. After everything we've been through, I just want peace."

"Fat they're not there 'cause I don't trust you. I put them up so I

GLITZ

can make sure y'all good since you still ain't tryna come home," he griped, and she didn't miss the annoyance in his tone.

"And you just so happened to be watching when she walked in?" His laughter filled her ears, and she rolled her eyes.

"I get an alert every time somebody pull into that driveway. I'm not taking them down so let it go. You let somebody else kiss you and I'ma twist your lips off your face."

She placed Story on the couch. She bent over, pulled her pants and panties down, and smacked her ass.

"You see that? 'Cause that's exactly what you can do kiss my ass." She picked Story up and got on the couch.

"I do more than kiss it, Fat, that's why yo' ass crazy now. Let me see it again."

"Nope. Bye, I love you."

"I love you more. Kiss my baby for me. I'll be there in a couple of days."

"Hurryyy, Rainbow misses you," Signy cooed. He smacked his lips, imitating her and she fell out.

"Okayy me and Fat miss you, too."

"I miss y'all too, baby girl, so much. Y'all call me so I can see y'all when my daughter sleeping." Signy and Stprix made up and hadn't gotten enough of each other. The two weeks they were in Nashville, Story was with her grandparents while they were out enjoying each other's company and in the house, having sex.

"Nope, if you miss us, come fill us up right now," Signy challenged and listened to him groan in her ear.

"You dirty, Fat." He ended the call, causing her to laugh.

Signy changed Story then fed her and rocked her to sleep. She held her for almost a hour before walking upstairs. She pushed her bassinet in the bathroom and placed her in it before undressing.

She took a quick shower and got out, brushed her teeth, and washed her face. Signy put on a robe and carefully pushed Story into her bedroom. Signy got dressed in a black silk gown that stopped in the middle of her thick thighs. She turned the TV on and picked a sleeping Story up. Signy pulled the covers back and carefully climbed under the covers with her on her chest. In no time, Signy was sleeping. Signy awoke, looking down at the head in between her legs. The amount of pleasure that flooded her body had awakened her from her slumber. Stprix had his entire tongue inside of her while he stroked her clit. She was already ready to fall over the edge. Stprix could see it in her face as they stared at each other.

"Don't be too loud," Stprix warned.

Ever since she told him to come fill her up, it was all he could think about. He called his pilot an hour after he couldn't get Signy off his mind. He licked her up and down over and over, making sure to pay extra attention to her clit. Signy's eyes rolled to the back of her head as she covered her mouth with her hand as she came hard. Stprix hovered over her with a wet face and slid into her.

"This what you wanted, huh?"

Thanks to the lamp being on, they were able to stare into each other's lust-filled eyes.

"Pull out, I'm not having a another baby," Signy moaned out, causing him to frown.

"Fuck you mean?" Stprix slowed down his strokes and placed his palms on each side of her head.

"Prix, don't start. I've been pregnant two years in a row," she whined.

"That last year don't count, you didn't even know you was pregnant," he argued as he slammed into her. She met his thrust, hoping to get off the subject of having another baby.

"Fat, so you ain't gon' give a nigga another pretty ass lil' girl?" He flipped her over onto her knees and wrapped his hand in her hair.

"Yesss!" She moaned a little too loudly as he slid into her, going balls deep.

"That's what the fuck I thought." He smacked her ass. She threw her ass back at him at a dangerously fast rate, and he helplessly watched her ass slam into him. His bottom lip was tucked in between his teeth while she took his soul.

"Got damn, Fat I'm finna… shit, girl," he moaned as he gripped her waist. They came together, moaning uncontrollably in the process.

"Stprix, what did I tell you?" Signy snapped.

"Ain't no way you thought I was gon' be able to pull out. My legs numb as a bitch." He spooned her while placing kisses all over her back.

"Thanks for coming. I missed you." Signy turned to face him.

"I missed you too, Fat." He pressed his lips into hers as he pulled her body against him. She buried her face in the crook of his neck.

"Even though you only came for pussy."

"I did I ain't even gon' lie," Stprix admitted, causing her to laugh. The knocking at the door startled Signy.

"What!" Stprix called out.

"I need a bottle," Stox yelled from the other side.

Signy got up and went into the bathroom to wash her hands before quickly making Story a bottle. She pulled on a floor length robe then rushed to the door.

"Hey, son!" Signy opened the door with the biggest smile on her face.

"What's up Ma. She started whining so I figured she was hungry." Stox hugged Signy, and she kissed the top of his head. Signy took Story to make sure she was dry and then she passed her back to her big brother.

"Or did you want me to take her?" Signy asked, and he frowned, looking just like Stprix.

"We good. He the one need your attention, he been in a bad mood for three days." Stox looked past Signy at Stprix, who was in the bed under the covers watching their exchange.

"Fuck you, lil' nigga," Stprix smirked, causing Signy and Stox to laugh. Stox walked off with Story in his arms. Signy closed and locked the door.

"Why you tell me not to be loud? I thought Rainbow was in here or something."

"You be loud as fuck and these cheap ass walls haven't been sound proofed."

Signy untied her robe and walked towards him. She let it hit the floor when she reached the bed. She climbed in the bed and got under the covers. She laid on top of him and he wrapped his arms around her.

"Who all here?"

"Your favorite four sons," Stprix replied, and she sat up, looking at him like he was crazy.

"Don't do that. I love all of them but you know Gabriel and Monique be feeling a type of way and that's 'cause of yo' ass."

"Y'all need to have a conversation though 'cause I don't like splitting my kids up."

"You're not still fucking them, are you?"

Stprix smacked her ass cheeks then firmly gripped them. He squeezed until he saw that familiar look of lust cloud her eyes.

"You know I'm not fucking nobody but you and haven't fucked nobody since you left a nigga."

"Okay, I'll talk to them hoes, but I'm swinging if they don't keep it cute," she said as he flipped her on her back.

"I created a monster." Stprix slid into her, filling her up once again.

8

Monique was in the middle of the dance floor with her best friend, Kenzie. They were having a time. Stetson was out of town with Stprix and his siblings, so she was kid free. Someone bumped into her, and she turned around ready to snap until she saw who it was.

Echo stood before her, looking fine as ever. He was dripped in Gucci from head to toe and looking like a light show.

"My bad, sexy." He showcased his mouthful of ice, lowkey making her panties wet. Emery Roland was forbidden fruit and one of Stprix's opps.

"I think you did that on purpose," Monique accused as he looked her up and down. She was dressed in a leather black tube-styled dress that stopped in the middle of her thick thighs. It had a split on one side. Her makeup was flawless. Her red matte ombré lips stood out the most against her dark complexion. Her hair was styled in a silver bob that brought out her round face. Three dainty tennis chains decorated her neck, matching the bracelets that adorned her wrist.

"What you gon' do about it?" Echo stepped even closer to her, invading her personal space. Monique couldn't help the goosebumps that formed on her skin. They stood in a sea of people in an intense stare off.

"Have a good night." Monique turned and walked off to put some much needed space in between them.

Her and Kenzie walked out the club. They walked towards their cars that were parked side by side. Monique got inside her black Lamborghini and brought it to life. Kenzie peeled out, and Monique pulled her seatbelt on. She looked ahead, and Echo was standing there blocking her path. She didn't want to die no time soon, but if Stprix found out about them conversing, he just might murder her. He walked around to the passenger side, and she thought long and hard about unlocking the door but against her best judgement, she did. He got in, and she turned to face him.

"Nigga, what you want? Me and Stprix not together. We not fucking. So leave me out of y'all's bullshit, please."

"This ain't got nothing to do with nobody but me and you, Monique. I think you pretty as fuck. I want to get to know you better."

"My baby daddy ain't gon' like that though." Monique wasn't trying to get on Stprix's bad side; she didn't care how fine Echo was.

"Don't that nigga got a bitch? I ain't tryna talk about your baby daddy. I want you."

Monique thought about Stprix and Signy. Signy was right about one thing; ever since she had been in the picture, she hadn't gotten her baby daddy back. For years, Monique had only slept with Stprix. Her son was almost twelve, and Stprix was the only man she had slept with since she had Stetson. He didn't force her to only sleep with him but she did it, hoping he would see how much she loved him and wanted to be with him. After all of that, Stprix hadn't touched her since Signy left him.

"How do I know you genuinely want me though?" Monique quizzed.

"Shid, 'cause I'm telling you. I'll give you a million up front and if you feel like I ain't genuine, then you got a million dollars out of the equation."

Her phone rang with a call from Stetson, and she answered.

"Ma, why you not at home? I just checked your location." Stetson's voice filled her vehicle, causing them to laugh.

"I'm grown, and I'm your parent. I'm about to go home. What you doing? I miss you," Monique cooed.

"I miss you too and nothing, playing the game," Stetson replied.

"Okay, son, be good and no fighting with your brothers. I love you."

"Aight. I love you more let me know when you get in the house. Don't forget," Stetson demanded, and she hung up in his face.

"He ain't gon' send his shooters looking for me is he?" Echo teased.

"He might, you see he don't play about his momma. Get out my car, nigga. I'm sleepy and drunk." Monique turned the radio up slightly, hoping he would take a hint.

"Let's go chill."

"Fuck I look like to you? It's two o'clock in the morning."

"I know what time it is. We can chill in the car pull off and find us a nice lil' spot or you need me to drive?"

She turned her head, looking at him like he was crazy but she pulled off. He turned the radio up while she navigated them to their unknown destination.

"I don't know where to go." Monique glanced at him as he rolled a blunt. He pointed to the condos on the corner.

"Who lives here?"

"This one of my spots."

"Echo," Monique warned.

"We don't have to get out. Damn, you scared of a nigga?" He asked as she pulled up outside of the gate.

"Should I be?" She asked, and he leaned towards her invading her space. She momentarily took her foot off the brake. She quickly slammed her foot on the brake, jerking him forward.

"Chill, Pretty, you in the hands of a real nigga. Ain't nothing gon' happen that you don't want to happen and you safe anytime you with me and without me if I fuck with you." He let her window down and tapped the code into the gate.

"Sounds good." Monique stiffened even more when his face got close to hers. Their lips touched, igniting a flame within side of Monique.

She turned her head to the side, and they curiously stared at one another. A horn blaring behind them caused them to snap out of their trance.

"Move, I can't see."

"Give me a kiss first or I ain't moving." Echo inched even closer to her as the horn honked again. He let the window down and stuck his head out.

"Blow that got damn horn again, and I'ma blow yo head off." Echo looked back at the car, shooting the driver a sinister look. The man quickly tossed his hands up in surrender. Monique grabbed the back of his shirt, pulling him back in the car.

"Come on, Pretty. You about to make a nigga catch a body 'cause you playing and shit." Echo had the audacity to look at her like everything was her fault.

"I must attract crazy muthafuckas 'cause what?" Monique leaned up and pressed her lips against his. He gripped her neck and deepened their kiss. Monique couldn't believe she had a total stranger's tongue in her mouth. In fact, he wasn't a stranger he was someone who had robbed and shot Stprix before.

He pulled away, and her nipples were pressed against her dress. She hadn't had sex in so long, and he was about to awaken the nympho inside her. He let the window down again and pressed the code in once more before taking his seat on the passenger side. Monique pulled off and he guided her to the parking garage. They parked in a secluded spot.

"I have to pee."

"We can go upstairs. You good with a nigga that's on my daughter. I'm not gon' hurt you. Me and that nigga don't fuck with each other but it ain't no smoke." Echo got out, walked around to her side, and opened the door.

She hesitantly got out. He tossed his arm over her shoulder like they were a couple and led her inside. Monique was a nervous wreck,

GLITZ

thinking someone would see her and report back to Stprix. She didn't breathe a sigh of relief until they were inside.

"Make yourself at home. The bathroom is down the hall."

Monique walked to the bathroom and looked around for any signs of a woman but she didn't find any. She quickly used it then washed her hands. She walked out and found him smoking on the balcony. She walked outside, taking in the beautiful view of the city. She pulled out her phone and snapped a picture.

"Here." He held his blunt out to her.

"I haven't smoked in years." She accepted it from him, put it up to her lips, and took a pull from it. They silently passed the blunt back and forth before walking back inside.

"I'm high as fuck." Monique laughed, causing him to laugh. They sat down on the couch, and he turned the TV on. He scrolled on his phone and found them a late night spot to order some food.

"Any time you want to smoke pull up on a nigga."

"No. I'm here now, and I'm not coming back. I don't got time for no drama. I'm trying to turn over a new leaf in my life." She took her shoes off and crossed her legs. She had been on one and mad at everyone around her but herself. She loved Stprix but she was starting to love herself more.

"I respect your loyalty. I need that."

"Whatever. This doesn't look lived in. What is it your bachelor's pad?"

"Nah. I just got it so I could have something in the city. I live almost an hour away, so I be needing somewhere to sleep at when I'on feel like driving home. You the only person that's been here," Echo admitted.

Monique nodded her head.

"So you ain't gon' let a nigga take you on a date?" He asked, rolling another blunt.

"What I say?!"

"Well that means I have to make a lasting impression on you tonight."

* * *

It had been three days since Monique left with Echo, and he had been on her mind. She wondered if that was because she hadn't been entertaining, hoping Stprix would double back like he always did, but she was wrong. She knew Stprix wasn't thinking about her. The door opened to her salon and a man walked in.

"I'm looking for Monique." The man looked around, and Monique stood from behind her station and greeted him. She signed the paper on his clipboard, and he held the door open for the three workers that had bouquets of roses in both of their hands. She showed them where to put the flowers with all eyes on her.

Once they left, she walked to the back to her office for privacy and opened the card. She was slightly disappointed. She was hopeful that Stprix sent the roses but they were from Echo.

You been on my mind. Can I take you out, sexy? Text me 567-645-7888

Monique saved his number in her phone against her better judgment. She wanted to think about dealing with Echo fully before she did something she couldn't take back. She walked out and took pictures of the flowers before sitting down to finish her client's nails. She was the proud owner of *Mo Nail's* it was her pride and joy. She had six other nail techs that worked alongside her that paid her a weekly booth rent. She went to school for nails ten years ago, and she had been doing them ever since.

"That was really sweet of Stprix," Nikki, one of her regulars, pried.

"Honey, I guess. You like your nails?"

"Yess thank you, Mo. How much I owe you?" Nikki held her hand out so she could get a better look at the leopard print Frenchies.

"Eighty." Monique focused on her phone. She uploaded the picture of the six dozen roses to her Instagram story. Nikki handed her a hundred dollar bill. "Thank you, Nik. I'll see you in a couple of weeks and yo' ass is getting a fill-in so don't even try it."

"You make me sick." Nikki walked out while Monique picked up her phone that was ringing with a call from Stprix.

She silenced her phone while she cleaned up her work space. She was finally finished with her work day after doing six clients. She said her goodbyes to her team and walked out the door, getting in her red Range Rover. Stprix called back, and she answered.

"What you doing?"

"What do you want, Stprix?"

"Really, Mo? You hard on your baby daddy."

"Nah, my baby daddy hard on me. What is it? I haven't talked to you in a long time so to what do I owe the pleasure?"

"Meet me at your house," he demanded and ended the call.

She sucked her teeth but she pulled off and headed in the direction of her mansion that was fifteen minutes away. She pulled in her wrap-around driveway behind Stprix. He got out and opened the back door.

Monique watched in envy as he got Story out of the backseat. She got out and went and unlocked the door. She sat her purse on the table in the foyer and kicked her shoes off. She headed for the kitchen and washed her hands. Then, she prepared her a glass of wine. Her phone rang with a call from Stetson as Stprix walked in the kitchen. She answered, placing him on speaker.

"What's up, son?"

"Hey, Ma! My daddy sent you them flowers today?" Stetson pried, and Stprix's eyes went to her.

"Stetson, what the fuck I tell you about getting in my business? When I block you off my Instagram, don't say shit." Monique hung up in his face, and Stprix frowned.

"Why the fuck you talking to him like that? Who sent you flowers? Now I wanna know."

"Why? You got a bitch. I'm not your business no more, you've made that clear. What you want to talk about?"

Stprix walked around the island, standing in front of her. They stared at one another. He grabbed the front of her scrubs, swooping her off her feet. He hemmed her up against the refrigerator.

"Who sent you flowers?" He repeated. The sound of Story's cries startled them. Stprix let her go and in that moment she was thankful for Story's presence.

He left the kitchen, and she picked up her glass of wine and followed him. She watched him pick her up and smiled when Story instantly stopped crying.

"Awww lil' mama spoiled." Monique sat beside them on the couch. "She looks just like that bitch." Monique rubbed her cheek soothingly.

"Don't be disrespectful, Mo," Stprix warned.

"Wow, you really love her."

"I love you, too. I ain't mean to make you feel less than, my apologies if I did. You know how I feel about you. You been my safe space for a while, and I want you to know I appreciate you and everything you've ever did for a nigga."

"Awww thank you, baby. I appreciate that. I love you more. Can I hold her?"

Stprix passed Story to Monique and watched their interaction. Monique held her up, making baby talk and Story was eating it up.

"We should've had another baby."

"Don't make me mad, Mo. I'm trying to be nice."

"Sorry I'm not trying to. She got me having baby fever. Look at her hair she looks like her brothers, too. Take a picture of us and send it to her mammy." Monique had snuck out of town and terminated one of her pregnancies. Stprix didn't talk to her for months or sleep with her.

"Who sent you flowers, Mo?"

"I don't know," she lied.

"You do know I'ma find out, right? I'ma make it my business since you being sneaky about it."

His phone rang with a call, and she was thankful for the distraction until he answered for her.

"What's up, Fat?"

Monique couldn't hear what Signy was saying but she was ear hustling.

"Nah, I'm about to drop her off. We at Monique's house right now. I love you. I'll call you when we leave."

Monique rolled her eyes after hearing him confess his love to her.

"I wanted to talk to you about you, Pooh, Kay, Nya, and Signy sitting down so y'all can have a conversation without all the drama. I don't like that whenever I'm trying to travel with all my kids, you don't want Stetson with Signy. I just told her where we was, and she didn't trip. I'm asking for the same thing from you, Mo, please."

"I'll sit down with them, and we'll go from there, Prix."

He kissed her forehead and took Story from her. He kissed Story's lips and she laughed, causing them to join in on her laughter. Monique knew she had to move on from Stprix but she really didn't want to. For over eleven years, he spoiled her rotten. Before him, she only had two other partners but none of them could compare or compete with Stprix Alexander.

9

Monique was in her office, taking a much-needed break. One of her nail techs called out sick, so she was doing both of their clients' nails. Her next client wasn't due for two hours, and she was on the couch under her heated blanket smiling at her phone. She had finally given Echo a chance. She texted him three weeks ago after Stprix and Story left her house. She was starting over fresh. Every week he took her on four dates out of the city in his helicopter, and she was swooning.

"Baby, I'ma call you back. I got something that's real important that needs my attention."

"Nigga, what?" She snapped. He laughed in her ear before hanging up in her face. There was a knock at her door, and a couple minutes later, her receptionist opened the door.

"I know you heard me knocking, Mo. I have a visitor here for you."

Monique perked up at that. Stella her receptionist stood to the side, and Echo walked in, holding a bouquet of roses and a bag of food in his hands. Stella walked out, closing the door behind herself. Monique jumped up and hugged him.

"Damn, bae, can I put this shit down. A nigga missed you, too. I'm glad to know I'm growing on your mean ass." She stuck her lips out, and he laughed before pressing his lips into hers.

She let him go, and he sat the stuff down on the table in front of her couch and picked her up. She wrapped her arms around his neck while he held her ass cheeks. She wanted to ask him why he had come to her place of business but she didn't care. He was a welcoming distraction from Stprix.

"You think I'm mean?" She pouted.

"Hell yeah you be mean as fuck sometimes." He sat down on the couch and she climbed off him and sat beside him. He removed their food and they ate together. Monique disposed of their trash, then they laid on the couch together. She laid on top of him so they both could fit.

"What time yo' next client?"

"I have two hours to myself. Take a nap with me. They'll let me know when she gets here," Monique replied groggily. In no time, she was sleeping. Echo wasn't trying to but he nodded off as well.

A couple hours later, there was a knock at the door. Monique got up and opened the door, sticking her head out.

"You're six o'clock is here. I told her to give you a minute."

"Okay thanks, Stella." Monique shut the door and turned to see Echo still asleep. She went into the bathroom and got herself together then she rushed out to get started.

"Hey, boo! I was back there knocked the fuck out. What you getting today?"

"You can do a freestyle set and you good, love."

Monique turned the TV up and they talked while she did a freestyle set. She loved when her clients trusted her creativeness. Forty-five minutes later, she was done and the client loved them.

"This is why can't nobody else do my nails! They so tea! How much I owe you?"

"One twenty-five and thank you so much." Monique checked her phone as the door swung open. Her next client walked in, and she sent her to wash her hands. Her client in her chair paid her one hundred and fifty dollars before leaving.

Her next client got a gel manicure, and she was glad because it took her twenty-five minutes. She went to the back to check on Echo. He was sitting up on the couch, rolling a blunt.

"You finna leave me?" She sat down beside him.

"What time you gon' be done? I gotta go get my lil' girl."

"I just got one more. She should be pulling up now."

He tucked the blunt behind his ear and pulled her into his lap.

"You gotta get your son tonight? If not pull up to the condo and let me know when you outside so I can come get you."

Echo was turning out to be everything. She was genuinely feeling him and the feelings were mutual.

"I want to fuck and suck on you," she admitted, causing him to lick his lips in anticipation.

"I'm finna go spend time with my lil' girl and drop her back off. Hurry up." He gripped her throat and kissed her with so much passion, she couldn't breathe when he pulled away.

"Damn, nigga." She moaned lightly.

"I'ma about to eat you alive," he whispered in her ear before kissing and sucking her neck. He smacked her ass and she stood and he got up behind her hugging her from behind. Then he walked out, leaving her hot and bothered.

* * *

MONIQUE, Kenzie, and Gabriel were out at the club having a ball.

"Bitch, you glowing. You been fucking our baby daddy?" Gabriel questioned with her hands on her hip.

"Nope, fuck yo' baby daddy. I'm about to have another baby daddy." Monique picked up her bottle, pouring her a shot.

Gabriel and Kenzie shared glances, and Kenzie shrugged. Monique wasn't telling nobody about Echo until she was ready. He made love to her then fucked her like a slut, and she enjoyed every second and minute of it.

"That's clearly a new dick glow. She's holding out on me and you," Kenzie spoke up.

"I'll tell y'all when the time is right. Right now, I just want to enjoy the nigga and his big ass dick." Monique bit her bottom lip just thinking about the way Echo tossed her all around his condo.

Her phone vibrated in her hand as if she thought him up. She smiled hard as ever after realizing he was in the same club with his eyes on her.

"You need to find me a man, bitch," Gabriel whined.

"Gabby, you want our baby daddy."

"Bitch and you do, too!" Gabriel snapped.

"No. I don't. I wanted that nigga but new dick will have you forgetting just how good that old dick was," Monique sang, and Gabriel smacked her lips with a mean eye roll.

Monique's phone vibrated in her hand again. She walked off without telling them where she was going. She headed for the side door of the club and walked out. She found Echo's matte black G-Wagon with tents so dark she couldn't see in. She got in on the passenger side.

"What's up, baby? What you got on?" He frowned.

"Clothes. Heyyy, I missed you," she cooed.

"I missed you too. Don't wear no shit like that out again, this looks like something for my eyes only." He tugged at the top of her fire red all-lace dress.

"If it was for your eyes only, my nipples and pussy would have been out."

He pulled her into his lap and rubbed her back soothingly.

"I wanna toss you in my back seat and pull off," he said as she straddled him, wrapping her arms around his neck.

"How long you finna be in there?"

"I don't know. You finna go?"

"Yeah." He buried his face in her chest. He pulled her dress down, exposing her titties. Monique dropped her head back as he licked and sucked her nipples.

She was so glad that she had given him a chance. He was everything that she needed and some.

"Where you about to go?"

"To the condo."

"I'll be over there."

"Don't take forever, I need that." He kissed all over her chest before pulling her dress back up.

"Okay," she said shyly. He reached into his pocket and pulled out two stacks of bills and handed it to her.

"You drove?" He asked, and she nodded.

"Let me know if you need me to come back and get you. Call me when you leave so I can make sure you straight."

"Okay, baby." She gripped his chin and kissed his lips lovingly. She turned in his lap, and he wrapped his arms around her waist. She pulled down the visor and checked her makeup in the mirror. He kissed the back of her neck then her shoulder blade.

"I got to get out of here before I tell you to pull off." She opened the door, preparing to get out but he held her tighter.

"You got a hour, nah forty-five minutes." He looked down at the time on his Patek. She nodded her head in agreement. She got out and still didn't want to leave. He bent his head, and she kissed his lips.

"Be careful." She turned around and locked eyes with Fox, who was standing across the parking lot.

"Bae, you good?"

"Y-yeah, go on I'll see you in a minute." She walked inside, and Fox was right behind her.

"I really want to act like I didn't see that shit." Fox followed her as she continued her stride, hoping that he got the picture.

"Do what you got to do." Monique turned to face him before walking off altogether.

10

Stprix and Fox were in the basement of Fox's home shooting dice.

"Guess who I seen getting out of that nigga Echo truck." Fox said, and Stprix looked at him strangely.

"I'on give a damn about who getting in and out of that nigga shit."

"You gon' care about this."

"Nigga, spit that shit out and quit playing."

"Monique."

"Fuck you mean Monique?" Stprix stood frowning. He just knew there was no way his Monique would be getting out of one of his enemies vehicles.

"You can't be right."

"I recognized the nigga truck when I walked outside. You know you can't see through his tents but anyway the door opened, and she was sitting in that nigga lap. His hands was wrapped around her waist. Then, she got out and they kissed. She turned around and saw me and froze the fuck up. She walked in the club, and I followed her. I said I really wish I didn't see none of that, and she said do what you got to do."

Stprix walked towards the steps, taking them two at a time. He loved Monique a lot; he just happened to love Signy more. He walked outside and got in his truck. Fox opened the passenger door, irritating him even more than he already was.

He pulled off and sped towards Monique's house. He unlocked the door and walked inside. He yelled her name and when she didn't answer, he called her phone. She pressed ignore, and he called back to back until she texted, asking him *was everything okay?*

He quickly texted her back, accusing her of being with Echo. He saw the dots appear letting him know she was texting him back but just as fast as they appeared he watched them go away. He couldn't believe Monique of all people would do him dirty, but he knew Fox would never lie to him.

"Signy ain't gon' like you flipping out, just take yo' ass home."

"I ain't tryna hear that right now." He dialed Monique's phone again, and she pressed ignore. She texted him, making his blood boil.

Mo: We can talk when you calm down.

He read her message and texted back two words and seven letters: *fuck you.*

* * *

MONIQUE HAD BEEN a nervous wreck for days. Even still that didn't keep her away from Echo. Stprix texted her five days ago, and she had been out of the city at Echo's home. She pulled into her wraparound driveway behind Stprix. She only went home because it was time to get Stetson from him.

She got out and walked inside with an extra pep in her step. She was falling in love with someone other than Stprix, and it felt good because she never thought that was even possible. She walked around, looking for Stetson and Stprix but she couldn't find them anywhere. She pulled out her phone and dialed Stetson.

"Hey, baby, where you at?" She asked, walking in her bedroom.

"I'm at Granny's. Where you at?" He asked. She felt someone walk up behind her.

GLITZ

"I just got home. I'll be to get you in a minute." She turned around, coming face to face with her baby daddy.

"I want to spend the night, Ma. I'll be home tomorrow if that's okay with you? I love you."

"That's cool, son. I love you more." She ended the call, feeling like she was all alone with Stprix.

"You fucking Echo? That's the nigga that sent you them flowers to the shop when me and Stetson asked you about it?"

She closed her eyes and sighed. She wasn't ready to have that conversation with him, not then not ever.

"Yeah. It wasn't something I planned, it just happened. He bumped into me at the club trying to talk to me, and I wouldn't give him my number. So, he sent the flowers to the shop with his number. That same day you came over and cut me off for good, I hit him up. I like him, Stprix, and I don't want you to think that I was being spiteful even though that's what it seems like. I love you, but I love somebody else too, now."

"You dead to me." He walked out of her room and headed for the stairs.

"What am I supposed to do, watch you love somebody else you just met after I been waiting on you for years?" She followed him down the steps.

"You right, I dragged you along when I shouldn't have. I wouldn't have tripped about you moving on but, bitch, you fucking on the nigga that shot and robbed me!" He snapped, causing her to jump.

"I'm sorry. I swear it just happened. Please don't be mad at me."

"Make sure that nigga sending you twenty thousand a month 'cause I ain't. You want to act like a opp, I'ma treat you like one."

He walked out, slamming the door behind him. He got in his truck and pulled off. Monique had him in his feelings, he couldn't deny that. Echo was the son of one of Stprix's friends, which was the only reason he wasn't in the dirt.

11

Katelyn had just pulled up to Little Fox's program. She was supposed to ride with Fox but she had to work late. She was a NICU nurse, and she loved her job. She left work, rushed home, took a shower, and got herself together. Then, she flew across town to his recital. She walked in and looked around for Fox. She found him up in the front seated beside Azura. She found her a seat in the back and texted him. She blushed as she watched him a couple minutes later walk to the back, looking for her. She stood and met him halfway. She grabbed his hand and led him to where she was sitting.

"Hey, baby! You didn't have to come back here. I just wanted to let you know I was here."

"The fuck I didn't. You look good as fuck, give me a kiss."

She leaned towards him and pecked his lips. She wiped her gloss off his lips. They held hands while watching the children play their instruments. When Little Fox walked out, Katelyn began recording.

"Oh wow! He did such a good job!" Her and Fox stood, clapping along with everyone else in the room.

After it was over, they went to the cafeteria where they had finger

GLITZ

foods for the guest and children. Azura walked in and her and Katelyn locked eyes.

Azura rolled her eyes and headed in the opposite direction of them.

"Your baby mama big mad at me," Katelyn sighed, and Fox shook his head.

"Y'all will be okay. She ain't fucking with me either."

"I can't tell, y'all was just sitting in there looking cozy to me."

"Man, go on, Kay, you tryna start some shit I ain't entertaining, you know what it is." He frowned, and she laughed. They took a seat and when all the kids ran out, Little Fox ran to Azura, giving her a single rose then he found them.

"Good job, son. I'm proud of you." Fox stood, and they slapped hands before embracing.

Little Fox ran around to Katelyn, and hugged her, before he gave her a rose.

"Aww thank you, baby! You did such a good job tonight! I'm proud of you, too. You want to go get something to eat when we leave or you going home with your momma?" Katelyn asked.

"I'm going home with my momma but when I come back tomorrow, can you cook that chicken I like, please?"

"Anything for you. I'll even bake you a cake." Katelyn loved cooking like she loved sex.

She only worked three twelve hour shifts three days out of the week, so she had free time to try out new recipes and film for her YouTube channel. She was popular because she was Stprix's first baby mama. He didn't have social media but all of his baby mamas and his friends posted him from time to time. She had a million followers on Instagram and five hundred thousand subscribers on her YouTube where she blogged her everyday life. Her followers were rapidly growing because word was spreading that she was Fox's girl, and he was just as important as Stprix. He had been posting and tagging her nonstop now that their secret was out of the bag.

Little Fox hugged them both again then he walked towards his mother. Fox and Katelyn walked out hand in hand. He walked her towards her car.

"Where you wanna go eat at?"

"It don't matter."

"Okay, well you lead us somewhere. I'm following you."

He got in his truck and pulled out behind her. Five minutes into their ride, his gas light popped on. He called Katelyn and told her to find a gas station. He followed her orange Ferrari into the nearest gas station. He put his gun on his waist and got out. He went inside to get some water and her favorite candy. He paid for his gas and walked outside. He dropped his bag and reached for his Glock. There were two masked men standing on both sides of her car. He pulled the trigger, hitting the one on her side right between the eyes before putting a bullet in the back of the other man's head. He rushed towards Katelyn, and she looked panicked but perfectly fine.

"I don't know why I didn't pull off. It was like I just froze up," she said when he snatched her door open, making sure she was okay.

He pulled out his phone and called one of the police officers he kept on payroll. He arrived in ten minutes and shut the scene down. He called a coroner and had the body's removed. He went into the gas station, got the video, and went to stores close by. After questioning Katelyn and Fox, he let them go. Fox pumped his gas then got in his truck. He dialed Katelyn, who answered on the first ring.

"You good, love?" He asked.

"I'm okay. You want me to go to your house or my house?"

"I'm still taking you out to dinner. It's Thursday." He said like he hadn't just killed two people.

"Okay," she agreed, and he heard the smile in her voice.

"Aye?"

"Yeah?"

"I love you."

"I know. I love you, too." She hung up and silently drove towards his favorite restaurant. They parked and walked inside and were seated. Katelyn often thought about the first time they crossed the line. It was all her doing, and she didn't regret anything.

GLITZ

    Katelyn was in the house crying about Quan. Quan was her boyfriend of the last three years. He cheated on her and she had just found out. She was too busy crying that she didn't realize she had left the door unlocked. Fox walked right on in. He headed toward the sounds of her crying. Katelyn tried to hurriedly wipe her face but it was too late, he heard and saw her and all that did was make her cry even more.

    "Kay, what the fuck wrong with you?" He rushed towards her, kneeling as she laid on the couch sobbing. "You want me to call Prix?"

    "No!" She blurted out, and he could tell by the way she answered him that she had to be crying about her dude.

    "You in here crying about that bitch ass nigga, Kay? Sit yo' ass up." He pulled her up and wiped her face with his hands. She sniffled repeatedly, hoping to keep herself from falling apart.

    "He cheated on me." Her chest rapidly rose and fell, indicating she was about to start crying again.

    "Aye, man, calm down and stop all that got damn crying!" He demanded as she collapsed on him. Her arms wrapped around his neck, and he didn't know what to do with his hands, but he put his arms around her back and held her tightly. Even when she settled down, he continued to hold her.

    "I'm so embarrassed." She nervously laughed while still in his arms.

    "Don't be, fuck that nigga... he didn't deserve you anyway." He knew he should've let her go but she felt good. They had never been that close before because it was inappropriate.

    "Thank you." She held her head up, staring him in the face. Their noses were inches apart that's how close they were.

    "What are you doing here, anyways?"

    "I came to get the boys." He licked his lips.

    "They're not here," she said with her eyes trained on his mouth.

    She wanted him to make the next move, but he wouldn't because he was too loyal to Stprix, so she made it. She gripped the back of his head while he still had his arms around her and kissed his lips.

    "What you doing?" He asked but he never let her go.

    She kissed him a second time, and he opened his mouth, and invited her tongue in. She pushed him back and pinned him on the floor, straddling him while still in an intense lip lock with him. His hands went under her dress, *realizing she wasn't wearing panties. He rubbed her ass cheeks while she moaned into his mouth. She felt his dick growing under her. She removed it from his briefs and his Nike tech pants. She eased down on to his dick, and they had been locked in ever since that night.*

He had been protecting her since that moment and tonight proved he always would. A moment of vulnerability had caused her to sleep with her baby daddy's best friend but she was glad that she did. She would've never in a million years think she would end up with Fox but he was the end for her.

"What you over there thinking about?" Fox pried.

"You catching me crying that day."

"I'm glad I did 'cause you fucked me like you loved me, it wasn't no way I could stay away from you after that," he said, and she smirked.

His phone rang with a call, and he answered as the server walked up. She ordered their drinks and food while he talked to Stprix.

"She good she sitting across from me. Worry about yo' bitch, nigga. Mine good!" He snapped, causing her to blush.

"Fuck you!" Fox hung up and put his phone up.

"Y'all are crazy."

"Azoria want me to pick her up from Azura's when I leave."

"Okay, me and Kisha want to to go Miami this weekend."

Their server brought their food out and along with their drinks.

"You not going, you just went last weekend. You gon' make me think you got a nigga there that I need to go smoke. And we don't know what's going on. They could've just been some jack boys, but I want to be sure. "

She sucked her teeth in annoyance but she understood where he was coming from.

"Okay baby."

12

Signy was out at the store with Story, who was playing with her feet. She would be six months in a couple of days, and Signy was going all out. Her first child didn't make it past a day, so she wanted to celebrate Rainbow's six months of life. Signy turned, grabbing a bottle, and a lady being accompanied by two men stood too close to Story for Signy's liking. Signy grabbed the basket and pulled it close to her.

"I just wanted to see the bitch that's responsible for my sons death," The woman spoke, and the more Signy stared, she realized she had to be Stprix's aunt because she resembled his mother.

Jaquie walked up, pulling his gun out like they weren't standing in Target. Her men reached for their guns when the woman held up her hand, halting them.

"It was nice meeting you, Signy. Jaquie." She turned and walked away, and her men followed.

"Come on, we gotta go." Jaquie led them outside and made Signy get in the car on the passenger side while he strapped Story in. He got in behind the wheel and demanded she call Stprix while he pulled off.

Jaquie drove to the safe house Stprix had set up for them in the event they needed it. Jaquie knew Stasia being in Charlotte wasn't good for nobody. Signy let Jaquie do all the talking. She was a little rattled. She looked in the backseat at Story, who was sleeping without a care in the world.

"Let me know when y'all inside." Stprix hung up. Signy heard the anger in his voice. He was about to be out for blood, and she was sure of it.

Jaquie drove in circles the closer they got to the safe house.

"Turn your phone off, sis. Do it now," Jaquie demanded, and Signy did what she was told.

Once Jaquie felt like no one was following them, he drove up to the gate and placed his hand on the keypad. A few seconds later, the gate opened. They drove through, and Jaquie waited until the gate closed before driving up the driveway. He jumped out and unlocked the garage. Then, he got back in and drove in the garage. Signy reached in the back and unhooked Story, who was wide awake now.

"Wait here." Jaquie locked the door and went inside. Signy grabbed her purse, got her gun out, and put it in her back pocket.

She cradled Story close to her. She didn't know what was going on, but she didn't get a good vibe from the interaction with Melvin's mother. A couple of minutes later, Jaquie walked out and got them. He grabbed Story's seat and diaper bag. They walked in, and he gave them a quick tour of the five-bedroom mansion. She walked in the master suite and laid Story inside the plush rose gold baby bed. Stprix had everything they needed in the house plus some. He had thought of everything. There was a knock at the door.

"Come in!"

Jaquie walked in and handed her a phone.

"He knows we're here. Call him and nobody else, you understand?"

"I got it. Thank you, Jaquie, for always having my back even though I be hard on you sometimes."

"Always, and I'on pay you no attention, crazy girl, it's all love. Find you something to watch on TV or something, we're going to be here a minute. Rainbow good?" He walked towards her crib, and she was staring at him.

GLITZ

"Bow! Bow!" Jaquie rubbed her stomach and watched her kick her legs like crazy while laughing.

He walked out and closed the door behind him. Signy turned the phone on and it began to ring in her hand.

"Hello?" She answered, and Stprix's voice filled her ear, easing her worry. He didn't sound as angry as before but she knew her man.

"We're good, baby daddy. Your child is laying here kicking and screaming. How are you?"

"You know me, kiss her for me." He laughed.

"Yeah, I do, which is why I asked."

"I ain't tryna hurt my momma," he revealed.

"Call her and talk to her. She told me she hates the distance between you two. She also said every time she tries to come around, you make it known she's not welcomed. She wants you to come around on your own but her biggest fear is that you never will. I told her I wouldn't tell you but I think you need to talk to her about this."

"What she say to you?"

Signy was wondering when he was going to ask.

"I just wanted to see the bitch that's responsible for my son...then Jaquie walked up."

"Okay. I got some shit I need to take care of. If something doesn't feel right, trust your instincts. I love you."

"I love you more."

* * *

STPRIX MADE sure all his loved ones were tucked away somewhere safe. Outside of his Ghana home, he had safe houses in different states. He sent everyone on a road trip where they were to change cars every three hours until they got to their destination. Stasia approaching his family left a bad taste in his mouth.

Melvin's funeral had been held in Ghana, and Stprix didn't show up or send a flower because he wasn't sorry. Melvin had disrespected his family and nobody was ever getting away with that. He didn't care who it was.

He sat down on the couch in his den and nodded off. He hadn't meant to. His phone rang with a call from Fox, who was in Charlotte.

"Everything is in motion," Fox let him know, and Stprix hung up. He pulled up the feed on his phone and impatiently waited on them to make their move.

He sent his jet to get Story and Signy in the middle of the night, hoping to get them past his aunt. He made Signy promise to keep in touch and she had been.

Stprix watched as the car backed out of Signy's garage and drove out the gate. He watched them the whole way to the clear port where his jet was waiting. He clutched his jaws in anger as men swarmed them and opened fire on them. Stprix jumped up with his hands on his head.

* * *

STPRIX LAID asleep in his man cave on the couch with his pillow over his face. He'd nodded off on accident.

"Alon?" He heard as someone stood over him. Only one person called him by his middle name and that was Millenia Alexander.

He snatched the pillow off his face and stared at her. He didn't know how or why she was there.

"Hey, baby. You okay?"

"What do you think?"

She sat down beside him on the couch. Their relationship had been nonexistent for a while. Stprix was thirty-four years old and had been on his own since he was seventeen. He created a lane for himself and never looked back.

"I'm sorry. I didn't think she would actually do that but a part of me knew she would. I'll take care of it," Millenia assured him, and Stprix's eyes went to her.

"What you mean you'll take care of it?"

"You know what I mean, Alon. I'll be in touch." She stood and headed for the door.

"You don't have to leave, Ma," Stprix let her know after recalling what Signy told him. He didn't want her to feel like she wasn't welcomed even though his soul was angry. His aunt thought he was the young boy he used to be but he wasn't, and she had fucked up.

"I need to, son. I'll be back as soon as I can. I promise," she said making him a promise that she planned on keeping. Stprix nodded his head hoping she was telling the truth. He stood and walked her outside. They hugged, and she kissed his lips before getting into the back of her awaiting truck.

Stprix walked in the house, locking the door behind him. He walked up the stairs and into the master suite. Signy laid in the bed while Story sat up beside her, clapping her hands to the music that played from one of her favorite shows.

"Daddy Rainbow!" Stprix called out, gaining her attention. She got on all fours and crawled towards the side of the bed where he was. He held his arms out, and she pulled herself up on him.

"Yo' momma must be pregnant. You just see that shit?" Stprix said to both of them.

"I'm not pregnant. I've never seen a man that has almost ten kids still trying for more, you gotta chill, BD."

He kicked his shoes off and picked Story up. He kissed her nose forehead and lips and she laughed. She was one of his most happiest babies. Signy walked into the bathroom and locked herself inside. She ran a hot tub of water and shook some Epsom salt inside. Then, she lit a bunch of candles all around the bathroom and dropped red rose petals all over the floor. She turned on the music. There was a knock at the door. She opened the door for Stprix, who was holding Story, who was on her way to sleep. He looked past Signy, taking in the scenery.

"What's this?"

"It's for you. I know you're tired and not sleeping. You can't take care of us like that so tonight. I want to take care of you." Signy took Story and laid her in her baby bed. She rubbed her stomach and in no time, she was sleeping.

Stprix walked up behind Signy as she watched their daughter sleep.

"I love y'all."

"We love you more, Daddy. Come on." She pulled him towards the door of the bathroom. She removed all his clothes until he was in his birthday suit. Then, she pulled him towards the tub. He got in while she grabbed his bottle of Paradis out of the bucket of ice and made them both a drink.

"I'll be back to wash you up just relax, okay?" She stood over him. He nodded his head in agreement.

Signy walked out, closing the door behind her. Then, she rushed out and put on the white lace lingerie set. She had handled her hygiene before he came up. Once she was dressed and wearing his favorite scent, she beat her face and put huge curls in her thirty-inch wig.

"Fat?" Stprix called out, and she could tell he was feeling his drink. She picked up her drink and tossed it back.

She walked in the bathroom, and his eyes roamed her entire body. His daughters had did her right, and he was appreciative.

"You look good as fuck, come here." She walked towards him, and he firmly gripped her hips.

"Stop, you're getting me wet," she moaned as his massive hands roamed her body.

"Let me see," he demanded, and she shook her head because he knew that wasn't what she meant. They shared a much needed laugh. Signy got on her knees beside the tub and washed him up.

He had set his aunt up to see if she would really kill his daughter because he already knew she would kill Signy, and she had failed miserably. While she thought Signy was still in Charlotte, she wasn't. She snuck away at the same time she thought she was ending her life.

"I love you, Signy. Thank you."

"You're welcome, and I love you more, Alon," she cooed.

"Don't call me that shit," Stprix griped.

Signy finished washing him up then she stood, holding a towel open. He stood and got out, and she dried him off before wrapping the towel around his waist.

"And I done told you I ain't your bitch." He smacked her ass as he followed her into the bedroom. She checked on Story to make sure she was still sleeping.

"I ain't made you my bitch yet, but I'm about to so hurry up," Signy demanded, and he smirked. The way she took his soul at times had him feeling like he had been bitched, and he needed that right now.

He pulled on a pair of sweatpants and grabbed his Glock. He walked around the home, making sure nothing looked out of place. Then, he rushed back upstairs where Signy was in the bed waiting on him.

"I put her headphones on so fuck me, nigga," Signy said as he climbed in bed, hovering over her.

"Fat, don't be doing my baby like that."

"It's just for a little bit, you know I'm going to take them off, and I don't want her out of my sight right now."

Stprix kissed her lips to distract her from their current reality.

13

Stprix was watching TV when Signy walked in the den with Millenia behind her with Story in her arms.

"Hey, baby you got company." Signy walked off, and Millenia sat down on the couch across from him.

Story cried and reached her arms for Stprix when she saw him. He chuckled as his mother looked on in bewilderment.

"Ohh, I see she's a daddy's girl. Gon' lil' girl," Millenia sat her on the couch, and she crawled really fast to him. She crawled into his lap and pulled herself up.

"She looks like she's getting out of the way for another baby."

. . .

"Same shit I said ain't that right daddy's baby." She grabbed his cheeks and kissed his lips.

"Thank you, baby." He hugged her little frame while Millenia looked on.

Stasia could have robbed her son of that moment or her, but Stprix was thinking two steps ahead like she had taught him and she was thankful to experience the moment with him.

"I just wanted to tell you to your face, you no longer have to worry about your aunt."

She passed him a phone and he watched his aunt right before her final moments.

"Thank you, Mama. I honestly didn't think you would be able to do it. Why did you?"

"Because, son, you're my child. I know I haven't been the best mother to you, but I would never sit back and let someone harm you or the people you love. Sister or not when it comes to you, anybody can go," she stated truthfully, and Stprix believed her. He always knew she loved him but it seemed like work came first, and the older he got he started to resent her for it.

"I'm sorry you had to do it but thank you, Nay. I really appreciate it."

. . .

She held her arms out for Story. Story stared at her in curiosity before she reached for her. Millennia's eyes lit up as she eagerly took her from Stprix.

"Hey, little girl. I'm your grandmother! Stprix, we have to change the dynamic of our relationship. I want to be in your life, I have for a long time, and my grandchildren's life. If that's okay with you?" Millenia kissed both of Story's cheeks.

"That's cool with me, Ma, but none of that half-ass shit especially with my kids."

"You got my word. I'll do better. I sent you twenty million dollars and put a million in each of their accounts including this little one." She made baby talk to Story, who looked on like she knew what she was saying with a huge smile on her face.

"For what?"

"Nigga 'cause I wanted to!" She snapped, and Stprix laughed. His mother was the reason he was a crash out because so was she.

* * *

Stprix was back home in Nashville. He had to force Signy and Story to come. He thought the whole situation with his family would have made her want to come but she put up a good fight.

. . .

GLITZ

It was twelve o'clock at night, and they had a house full of children. His phone buzzed, letting him know he had a visitor. He looked at the cameras to see Monique. His phone rang with a call.

"Bossman we got your baby mama down here. She's not too happy," Stprix's guard spoke into the phone.

"It's okay. I'm on my way down." Stprix hung up and looked at Signy, who was wondering where he was going.

"Monique at the gate. I'll be back."

"And? Why she can't get in? 'Cause she sholl walks her ugly ass in here when she feels like it any other time." Signy rolled her eyes just thinking about her.

"Not no more," he said, walking out the room. He walked outside and took the long walk to the end of his driveway. Monique was standing there on ten as she awaited his arrival.

"Why would you remove my name from your list? Can we talk, please?"

"Not right now."

"So, when?"

. . .

"When I feel like it. Get yo' ass off my property," he sneered and slightly felt bad when he saw her eyes fill with tears.

It had been a couple of weeks since he learned of her and Echo, and he couldn't deny it if he wanted to; he felt some type of way. It really bothered him when she didn't cut him off after he cut her off. His baby mama had moved on, and he didn't like it.

"Then, you gave everybody but me a million dollars when I'm the one that been holding it down for you the longe—"

"Nah, Kay have," he cut her off with a correction.

"Right, that's why she's fucking your best friend!" She spat as she opened the door to her truck.

"At least she ain't fucking a nigga that shot me, bitch. Get off my property before I forget that I produced with your unstable ass."

"Nigga, fuck you! You're just mad because I'm popping this pussy for another nigga that ain't you!" She laughed until he grabbed a handful of her hair, halting her from getting inside her G-Wagon.

"Say that shit again! I fucking dare you to." He had been fucking Monique the longest out of all his baby mothers. She was right; he was mad that she was fucking someone else.

. . .

GLITZ

"Nigga I said you just mad that I'm popping this pussy for another nigga," she boldly repeated, shocking herself and him in the process. "Now get the fuck off me. You dead to me too, nigga!" She yelled as tears spilled from her eyes. She couldn't believe the way Stprix was treating her. He let her go, and she turned around and smacked him hard across the face.

She got in her truck and slammed the door shut in his face. It wasn't that she needed the money but it was the principle of the situation.

"You know what's crazy, I wouldn't even talk to that nigga at first not even when he sent me a million dollars. You ain't gotta send me shit 'cause that nigga straight."

"Tell that nigga don't let his money run out trying to keep up with a hoe I made bougie." Stprix laughed as he walked up the driveway and into the house.

The sounds of his sons' voices filled the home. Stox, Storm, Shiloh, and Saturn were there, making his house feel like a home. He walked in the bar and poured him a double shot of Don Julio. Monique had pissed him off like only she could. He didn't know or want to know that she was fucking someone else but she made it her business to tell him. He took another shot then went upstairs to his room where Signy was. She was on the phone with a frown on her face. She walked past Stprix, bumping him hard as fuck on her way out.

He started to snatch her up but he was working on misdirecting his anger. So instead, he walked towards Story, who was on the bed watching Ms. Rachel with a Cheeto puff in her mouth. He got in the bed with her and laid down. She crawled towards him, propping her elbow up on his stomach. A couple minutes later, the door opened and all four of her brothers came in, and she went crazy.

"WAIT, let's see who she gon' go to first," Storm challenged.

THEY ALL STOOD on the side of the bed with their arms outstretched while cooing at her.

"COME ON, Rory! Come to your brabra!" Shiloh spoke first.

"COME ON BABY RAINBOW." Storm reached for her and she swatted at him, causing them to laugh.

"TELL them niggas you don't want them. Come on my baby," Stox cooed, and she reached her arms out for him. "We all know who her favorite brother is," Stox teased.

"DADDY THAT'S NOT FAIR. I didn't get to see if she would come to me." Saturn pouted. Saturn was his other baby.

"GIVE HER TO HIM, Stox, and quit all that whining, Sat," Stprix demanded. Stox passed Story off to Saturn, and she wrapped her arms around his neck.

SATURN HEADED towards the door and Stox was right behind him, causing Stprix to laugh. Shiloh walked out next.

. . .

GLITZ

"Pops, can you go get my brother, please? He said his momma not gon' let him come. Can you call her, please?" Storm begged.

"Who, Stetson?" Stprix quizzed as Signy walked in, looking like she was ready for war. Storm nodded his head.

"Okay, I will," Stprix promised, and Storm's eyes lit up in excitement. He ran out. Signy walked towards the door and locked it. Anytime he heard the doors lock, he got excited but when she stepped out the foyer, he knew she wanted smoke.

"Fuck I do?"

"You tell me?" She questioned with her hand on her hip.

"Fat, I ain't did shit." He got up and attempted to walk up on her, but she tossed her hand up halting him. She pulled out her phone and played the exchange between him and Monique.

"You sound pretty mad to me."

"I am mad. That nigga robbed me and fucking shot me in the chest. Fuck that bitch. I ain't got nothing for her."

"Stprix!"

. . .

"What, she called you?" He asked in disbelief.

Signy nodded her head, blowing him away. He didn't know how she even got Signy's number but he wasn't surprised. Whenever Monique was mad, she was a determined woman on a mission.

"So you're mad she's fucking someone else?"

"Yeah, I am."

"Is it because you just don't want her fucking or you're mad that it's someone that shot you?"

"You know why I'm mad, Fat. I'on even know why you approaching me with this bullshit, didn't shit happen. She mad and you letting her put that off on us. When have she ever called you let alone wanted to talk to you?"

"I'ma let you make it tonight but I know you don't forget that. I'll get out yo' way if you still want to fuck on your baby mamas. You better get yo' shit together."

She headed for the door but he grabbed her, wrapping his arms around her waist.

"I don't want nobody but you, and I damn sure ain't tryna fuck nobody that ain't you. You think I'ma fuck up what we got, again? I know what I got, and I ain't no fool."

. . .

GLITZ

Signy turned in his arms and looked up at him. He kissed her lips but she refused to kiss him back.

"Storm just asked me to get Stetson, you riding?"

"Nope but don't be gone too long. I might think you done fell into some pussy."

He mushed her in the face, causing her to laugh. She left the room, and he went in the closet to get dressed. He changed into an all-black Nike tech.

14

*S*tprix arrived outside of Monique's gate. He buzzed himself in and pulled in behind Echo's truck. *This bitch,* he thought to himself. He jumped out and walked up on the porch. He let himself in and walked inside to see all the lights off with a couple of candles burning. He walked up the stairs and headed for Stetson's room. He awoke him and placed his finger on his mouth.

"Get dressed and be quiet," Stprix demanded.

Stetson got up, looking around. He went into his closet and got dressed in the quickest thing he could find. Then, Stprix led him downstairs and out the front door. They got in his truck and left.

"What's up, son? You straight?"

"Momma brought a dude home tonight and then made me go in my room." He frowned. Even though Monique and Stprix weren't together anymore and hadn't been for a while, Stprix was the only man that Stetson had ever seen in his home.

Stprix knew she was mad and trying to get under his skin but she was going about it all wrong.

"Your momma is dating now, son. I know that's something you got to get used to. Hell, even I got to get used to it. I know you've only seen her with me, but me and her are not going to be together. I want you to come to terms with that. I'm with Signy, and she's dating someone. It'll take some time getting used to but you'll adapt."

"But why? Don't y'all love each other?" Stetson folded his arms across his chest.

"I love your mother very much but sometimes, love isn't enough to make two people be together. You'll understand that one day. Don't be too hard on your momma, okay?" Stprix said to Stetson even though he wanted to wring Monique's neck.

"You mad at her?" Stetson looked over at his father when they got to a red light.

"I am but that's not your concern, me and your momma will be fine. Anything else you want to get off your chest?" Stprix glanced in his direction before pulling off from the light.

"No sir, I'm ready to see my sister though."

. . .

"That's all y'all ass care about. What about Signy? You good with her and being around her? Or do we all need to have a conversation?" Stprix asked when he pulled up outside the gate. He opened it and drove in.

"We good, Dad, we talked. I like Signy. I feel bad for putting my hands on her," he admitted.

"Come on." Stprix got out and Stetson got out next. "Signy is good, son. I need you to do me a favor though?" Stprix asked as they walked up the steps.

"Huh?"

"Don't answer the phone for your momma and turn your location off."

"Dad." Stetson knew Monique well enough to know that wasn't a good idea.

"Trust me, okay. Can I trust you?" He asked, holding his hand out. Stetson shook his hand and passed him his phone. Stprix stopped sharing Stetson's location with her and blocked her number.

Then, they walked in and he passed him his phone back.

. . .

GLITZ

"Don't answer for numbers you don't know either," Stprix warned.

"Yes, sir," Stetson said as Signy rounded the corner. She walked up on them and hugged him, rocking from side to side.

"Heyyy, sonnnn! How are you?" She greeted, and Stetson blushed.

"I'm good. How about you? Where my sister at?"

"She's upstairs somewhere with your brothers. I'm glad you're here." Signy kissed the top of his head, and Stprix frowned as he ate it up.

"Me too! Dad don't be hating. She loves me too," he teased, and Stprix snatched him up, tossing him over his shoulder. He headed up the stairs and headed for the playroom where he knew everyone was.

Stprix placed him on his feet and put his finger up to his lips. Stprix walked in first, and Stetson was right behind him.

"Broski!" Storm spotted him first before his other siblings. They ran towards each other, slapping hands.

"Don't y'all muthafuckas be in here fighting. Stox, you want me to take your sister?" Stprix asked, and Stox got up and passed her off, shocking Stprix.

. . .

"Wait, let me see my sister, man." Stetson took her back from Stprix. He hugged and kissed her before giving her to Stprix. They left and went to find Signy, who was in Stprix's bedroom.

"Stankkkk! You got put out?" Signy walked up on them, and Story reached for her.

She walked her in the bathroom so she could bathe her. She ran her some bath water and undressed her. Stprix followed them, watching Signy in mommy mode. He loved watching her care for their daughter because life had robbed them of Saint.

"You a good mom, baby mama. I'm proud of you."

"Thank you, Stprix." She sat Story in her bath chair. Signy washed her up and rinsed her off before taking her out and wrapping her up in a towel. Story began to cry.

"Can you make her a bottle?" Signy asked as she held her against her chest, hoping to calm her down. When she settled down, Signy moisturized her chocolate skin tone before getting her dressed in her pajamas. Stprix took her and fed her. Then he laid her on his shoulder and burped her. He rubbed her back until she nodded off.

He gently laid her in her bed and walked in the bathroom where Signy was in the shower.

. . .

"I'M ABOUT to start charging you for these free peep shows," Signy said as he climbed on the marble countertop.

"I GOT IT." He pulled out a wad of bills from his pocket and tossed a handful of hundreds in the air.

"WHAT YOU WANT TO SEE, MISTER?" Signy walked towards the glass and pressed her nipples against it.

"BEND OVER, Fat, let me see it from the back." He gripped his dick, and she licked her lips.

SHE TURNED AROUND and pressed her ass cheeks against the glass. Then, she bent over while looking back at him. She spread her ass cheeks so he could get a better view. He walked up on the glass, pressing his body against it. She stood, walking towards the waterfall with her back to him and made her ass clap to the imaginary beat in her head and he was coming out of his clothes.

"YOU PITIFUL." She laughed as he stepped in the shower.

* * *

MONIQUE AWOKE the next morning wrapped in Echo's arms. She really liked him, and she felt like the feelings were mutual. She eased out of bed and went into the bathroom and handled her hygiene. When she walked out, Echo was sitting up in the bed on his phone.

"GOOD MORNING, BABY," he took his phone off his ear and greeted her.

. . .

"Morning!" She walked towards him and kissed the side of his mouth.

"I'm about to go check on my son. I'll be back. Everything you need is in the bathroom."

Monique pulled her robe on then left her room and walked upstairs. She walked in Stetson's room and when he wasn't there, she searched her six-bedroom mansion looking all over for him. She called his phone and when his voicemail picked up, she screamed his name.

"Bae, why the fuck you screaming like that?" Echo rounded the corner, after hearing the panic in her voice. She pulled out her phone and pulled up her surveillance footage to see a bunch of hours had been deleted.

"No! No! No! Stetson!" Monique yelled.

"Baby, what's wrong?" Echo walked up on her, and she recoiled from him.

"Don't touch me! Where is my son?" Monique asked, and Echo twisted his face up in confusion.

"What you mean, ma?"

. . .

GLITZ

"He's not in his room, and I can't find him in the house," she revealed while full blown panicking in the process.

Echo walked up on her despite her trying to fight him off. He wrapped his arms around her while she freaked out.

"On my daughter's life, I don't have nothing to do with him missing but on my life, I'll make sure he's returned back home to you safely," he vowed while rocking from side to side with her. He knew how crazy it must have looked because it was his first night over and Stetson had come up missing.

"I wanna be alone right now," she said, and he shook his head no. Monique didn't know who to trust. Echo seemed genuine but she didn't want to be naïve if he wasn't.

"I'm not leaving you by yourself," Echo stated. She pulled away from him and walked towards the living room where she dialed Stprix. She was dreading making the call to him because she was sure he was going to pull up on one hundred.

She nervously chewed her acrylics as she waited for him to pick up. When he didn't, she called right back.

"What, Mo?" He answered with an attitude.

"Stetson isn't here. Do you have him please tell me you do," she pleaded on the verge of tears.

. . .

"Fuck you mean he ain't there? Where is he?" Stprix snapped.

"He was here when we went to slee—"

"What you mean we?" Stprix quizzed as she walked to the kitchen. She fixed her some water because her mouth felt sand paper dry.

"I had company last night and before you say anything, he was with me the whole night," she admitted what he already knew and he hung up in her face.

"Fuck." She sat down at the island. She closed her eyes, and prayed that her son was safe and sound.

The sound of Echo walking in the kitchen startled her. She wanted to trust him but she didn't know if she should.

"Can you leave? I want to be alone."

"I need you to look at something," Echo ignored her even though she looked like she didn't want to be bothered with him.

"No, get the fuck out my house! If you had something to do with my son—"

. . .

"What? Aight, you got it don't call me nomo. I'm done fucking with you." Echo walked out the kitchen, and she was right behind him.

"You couldn't think I give a fuck about you being done with me when I'm looking for my child. My child that disappeared when I let you into my house."

Echo walked out the door then turned and faced her once more.

"Open yo' eyes, stupid ass girl." He walked off, and she slammed the door shut locking it. She slid down the door, and prayed harder than she ever had in her life. A part of her felt like Echo wouldn't kidnap her son, then again she was getting to know him so she didn't know what he was or wasn't capable of.

A message came through from Echo. He sent her a video. She watched it and jumped up with a huge smile on her face. He had a camera on his truck and every vehicle he owned. It was a video of Stprix walking by with Stetson. She felt so much better after learning her child was safe. She thanked the man up above then dialed Echo. He answered without saying a word and hung up in her face.

"Damn!" She yelled out loud to herself. She called him again but he pressed ignore.

Instead of calling a third time, she sent him a message apologizing. She nervously bit her nails as she waited for him to respond and when he did, she wasn't happy.

. . .

ECHO: Fuck you.

HE HAD SENT her the same message Stprix sent when he found out about them. Stprix was purposely shaking her life up because she had moved on. He knew she was going to accuse Echo, but he didn't care. She sighed in frustration hoping Echo would forgive her sooner rather than later.

15

*I*t had been three days since Stprix's stunt. Monique had been to the club two nights in a row. She was purposely trying to get a rise out of Stprix. He wanted to play games and forgot she was the queen of games. She hadn't called him since he hung up in her face.

SHE WAS on the dance floor with Kenzie, on their last dance for the night. Kenzie smacked Monique's ass while she bent over, shaking her ass on her. Monique had been turnt all night. She purposely went to Echo's partner's club because she knew he would be there. He hadn't said a word to her in seventy-two hours, and she felt some type of way about it. She felt bad for treating him the way she did, but she wanted him to understand where she was coming from. After-all he was a father.

"OKAY, let's go! I'm drunkkk!" Kenzie yelled to Monique.

. . .

"Okay. I can drive us." Monique faced her while still dancing.

A guy walked up and wrapped his arms around her waist. She turned, facing him thinking it was her man. She frowned at the sight of the stranger and tried to free herself from his grasp. She could tell he was under the influence of something.

"Let me go." She pushed his chest and his grip on her tightened.

"You pretty you tryna leave with a nigga." He slurred.

"Nigga, get yo' hands off of her!" Kenzie grabbed Monique, and he pushed her back.

Monique smelled the familiar scent of Echo. Unbeknownst to her, he stood behind her. He reached over her and smashed his gun into the dude's head. He continued to hit him until his homeboy grabbed him.

"Take yo' stupid ass home!" Echo yelled at Monique, who was now embarrassed. He really wasn't fucking with her, and it was her own fault.

Kenzie grabbed her hand and pulled her outside. They got in the car, and she drove Kenzie home, but instead of her going home, she went to his condo. She waited all of ten minutes, before she heard him coming in. She walked from the back to the front, and he was shocked to see her, but she was even more shocked to see him walking in with a woman. He looked like a deer caught in headlights. Long gone was the anger he had for her earlier; instead he looked like he had been caught with his hands in the cookie jar.

. . .

"You just like every other nigga." Monique laughed with a shake of her head. She walked past them, and he attempted to grab her but she dodged him and walked out the door. He followed her to the elevator while she impatiently waited for it to come to her rescue.

"I'm sorry. I didn't know you was going to be here."

"Enjoy your night," she shrugged as the elevator stopped and opened in front of her. She quickly stepped in and so did he, leaving the two of them trapped inside the steel box together. He hit a button and stopped It in the middle of them going down.

"My bad, baby." He walked up on her, and she pushed him back.

"Don't touch me, Echo!" She yelled as he inched towards her.

"Come get in the car with me, please." He pinned her body against the wall.

"No. I'm going home. I was wrong for accusing you that morning but put yourself in my shoes. I like you a lot but I'm not doing this." She pressed the button and the elevator began rolling again, and she got off when it stopped in the garage.

"Baby?" He called, out and against her better judgment, she turned and faced him.

. . .

"I LOVE YOU," he yelled as the elevator doors closed. She smiled but sighed right after. She got in her vehicle and drove home.

ECHO STARTED CALLING HER, and she refused to answer for him. She loved him but she couldn't talk to him now. He wasn't her man but seeing him bring a woman to the home that he promised was just for them stung. She went upstairs to her bedroom and undressed. She went into the bathroom and handled her hygiene then wrapped her body in a towel. She walked out to Echo strolling in like he had a key or paid the bills.

SHE ACTED as if he wasn't there while she got dressed. She got under the covers with her back to him. He kicked his shoes off and sat on the couch in the sitting area. He pulled a blunt from behind his ear and sparked it.

"I WAS JUST GOING to fuck. She ain't nobody to me," Echo admitted, and she rolled her eyes.

"YOU WAS GON' fuck her at the condo where I basically live. I got clothes and all type of shit there. On top of that you gave me a whole key. Did you forget or you just don't give a fuck?" She sat up as she yelled at him.

"IT'S JUST sex it ain't that deep. I didn't fuck her anyway so chill out."

SHE TURNED over and went to sleep with an attitude. The next morning, she awoke and he was gone. She went into the bathroom and handled her hygiene then she got dressed. She headed downstairs to

GLITZ

the kitchen and fixed her some much needed breakfast. She sat down and ate her food. The sound of footsteps echoed off the floors, and she was sure it was Echo coming back to get on her nerves. She didn't know how he had gotten in last night but she wasn't shocked. After dealing with Stprix for so long nothing surprised her.

Her visitor made their presence known, and she was shocked to find Stprix entering the kitchen. She picked up her glass of water and drank from it.

"So my son been gone for three days, and you been out at the club every night like you don't care."

"I guess I should have been home crying my eyes out. Is that what you wanted? Or did you hope that I would start beefing with my nigga when you took him. Oh, you don't think I knew you had him?" She laughed, making him even madder than he already was. She was familiar with that look of rage that washed over him.

"Aww you mad that I beat you at your own game. Get out of my house and don't come back ever. I'll be to get my son later."
   He snatched her up and wrapped his hand around her neck and squeezed. She clawed at his face as his grip tightened. He let her go and she bent over, coughing and gasping for air.

"Bitch, did you even think about how you made him feel when you brought a nigga home? For eleven years, he's only seen me and you together. And what 'cause you mad at me you fucking take it out on my see—"

. . .

"You know damn well I would never do that!" She yelled with what little bit of her voice was left.

"Think before you react. I keep telling you that."

She sighed because she didn't know she had made her son feel some type of way.

"Can I see him?" She asked Stprix because she knew the ball was in his court.

"You need to have a conversation with him. Don't make him uncomfortable trying to be petty with me 'cause I can be pettier," he promised as they listened to the front door open and close.

"I fucking heard you. Get out of my house," she sassed as Echo rounded the corner.

"Unc." Echo smirked as him and Stprix locked eyes.

"Lil' nigga, you ain't got another chance to fuck up with me. I don't play about her or my son. If you want to be in her life you need to always keep them safe and away from any bullshit you got going on. I don't care about your dad and me being friends when it comes to my family," Stprix spoke to Echo while Monique nervously chewed on her bottom lip.

. . .

"I got you." Echo nodded his head in understanding. Stprix walked away, and Monique followed him outside.

The passenger door opened, and Stetson got out and Monique rushed down the steps to hug him. She kissed all over his face, and he wrapped his arms around her.

"Hey, Momma!" Stetson laughed.

"Hey, babyyy! I missed you so much."

"I missed you, too."

"Go in and let me talk to your dad real quick." Once he was inside, she was left alone with Stprix.

"None of this was intentional but thank you for understanding and giving me your blessing."

"Yeah. Yeah. Yeah." He hugged her and kissed the top of her head.

She walked back in the house, feeling like a weight had been lifted off her shoulders. She found Stetson and Echo in the kitchen eating the breakfast she had cooked. She looked at Echo, and he tossed his head up at her and she rolled her eyes at him. She hadn't forgotten about catching him last night and even though they weren't together, she still felt some kind of way.

. . .

"What kind of game you got?" Echo asked Stetson.

"I have a PlayStation five and a Xbox. I want that new game that just came out yesterday."

"Aight, me, you, and your mama can go get it later."

"Bet!" Stetson slapped hands with Echo before rushing upstairs to his room.

"What you doing here?" She asked, and he frowned.

"We still on that?" He walked up on her and cornered her in between him and the kitchen counter. He kissed her neck, and she tried to push him away but he didn't falter.

"Yes! Have you taken other bitches over there to lay in my pussy juices?" She interrogated him, and he smirked.

"I haven't took nobody else over there, I promise, baby. I'll get rid of it if that'll make you feel better." He pecked her lips repeatedly.

"Are we okay?"

. . .

GLITZ

"Never better, baby. I told you I love you. I mean that shit," he said, and she smiled.

"I love you too! Don't fuck that up," she warned as he lifted her onto the counter.

"I'm not, baby." He grabbed her thighs while they stared into each other's eyes.

* * *

Gabriel walked through the Chanel store, shopping. She had been in a funk lately, and she didn't know why. Her sons were happy and healthy and they didn't want for nothing in the world, but she felt like something was missing. Stprix was her heart and their relationship had ended long ago, but at times, she still missed him. However, she had been passing time by forcing herself into her work. She was one of the top realtors in the state, and she was damn proud of herself and all her accomplishments. She went to Chanel to celebrate her selling her fiftieth home.

A man walked in, and they locked eyes but Gabriel quickly looked away. She continued her shopping and when she was done, she had six bags, three pair of glasses, and three scarfs.

"That's all you want?" The man asked while she was checking out. She turned and locked eyes with the handsome stranger again.

. . .

He let the saleswoman know he was purchasing her things while Gabriel drank him in. His skin was dark as midnight, and his eyes were light brown or hazel.

"Why you buying my stuff? You can't have my number and you can't take me out," she mouthed off as the lady boxed up and bagged her stuff.

"Shid 'cause I got it and it looked like you needed a real nigga to put a smile on your pretty face." He walked off, leaving his heavenly scent behind.

The woman handed her the bags as a woman walked in the store and greeted the man with a kiss to the lips.

"Wow." Gabriel walked out the store. She looked back and her and the stranger locked eyes again.

She mouthed the words *thank you,* and he nodded. His little stunt really did brighten her day whether he was taken or not. She walked outside and got in her Maybach. It was time for her to get her sons. Her phone rang, and it was her mother calling.

"Hey, Ma!"

"Hey, my baby! I hope you're still bringing my grandbabies over this weekend."

. . .

GLITZ

"I AM. I think I'ma go out tonight and tomorrow too."

"AS YOU SHOULD. You fine, single, and rich might I add. I'll be waiting on y'all to get here." Yolanda hung up, and Gabriel smiled.

She was a virgin when she met Stprix, so he had been her first love and the only man she had been with. They were in a relationship for four years until she caught him cheating more than once. However, even after that she continued to let him into her bedroom because he was all she knew. She had been in a situationship with her baby daddy for years just for him to end it for his newest baby mother. She was hurt and had been for a minute. She was trying her hardest to move on but it had been a journey.

SHE LAUGHED as her sons raced each other as they ran to her car. They got in, and Stprix Jr. kissed her cheek first and Stone was right behind him.

"HOW WAS SCHOOL?"

"IT WAS GOOD. I'M HUNGRY," Stone replied, while pulling his seatbelt on.

"I'M glad it's the weekend. I had a bunch of work this week. We still going over to Granny's right 'cause BJ told me he'll be there."

"YES, son. She just called to make sure y'all were coming."

. . .

Stone turned the radio up as Gabriel drove them to their favorite fast food restaurant and grabbed them, along with her momma and nephew, something. Then, she headed towards her mom's. They arrived, and her boys kissed her once more before getting out.

"You gon' be okay by yourself, Ma?" Stone asked as Junior rushed inside.

"Yes, baby. I'll be fine. You and your brother be good. Call me if you need me. I love you." She blew him a kiss.

"Okay, love you too." He closed the passenger door, and she watched him walk inside before pulling off.

16

Gabriel was at the club with her big sister, Gina. They were both kid free thanks to Yolanda. Gabriel went to the beauty shop and got her hair nails and toes slayed, after she dropped her boys off. Then, she went and got her makeup done and her pussy waxed. She was looking and feeling like a bad bitch. She was dressed in a leopard dress that was painted on. Her hair was styled in a forty-inch black wig that hung past her round ass that sat up on her back.

Thanks to her mother, she was every bit of a stallion. Gabriel was the color of toffee, and she had a body out of this world. She was a full size woman, that wore a size sixteen. She didn't have a waist, and her ass had a mind of its own. Her titties sat up perfectly thanks to the surgeon who did her breast lift after she had Junior. She had cat eyes with deep dimples in both of her cheeks and plump, pink lips that she had outlined in a black lip liner and painted in red matte lipstick that was coated in gloss. She was feeling herself and nobody could change that. She sat at the bar, ordering her a drink when a man walked up, offering to pay for her drink.

"I got it." The stranger from the Chanel store appeared out of thin air, and the man that was offering to buy her drink scurried like a water bug when you turned the lights on. That alone told Gabriel that Mr. Chanel was someone important.

"I should be buying you a drink. Thank you once again."

"You're welcome. You look different from earlier." He took her in from head to toe, and he liked what he saw.

"Is that a good or a bad thing?"

"Good, you look real good," he complimented, and she blushed. Once her drink was brought over, he turned to walk away until she gently grabbed him.

"You married?" She asked, and he stared at her in curiosity.

"Yeah," he revealed, and the little courage she did have to ask him for his number went away.

"Ohhh okay. Thanks for my stuff earlier and my drink." She half-smiled. He stared at her then walked away.

She stayed at the bar until Monique walked in. She got them a section and they started their turn up.

"Baby mama, you glowing," Monique beamed, remembering the time Gabriel called her out after meeting Echo.

"Anyways, Mo. But I did meet this nigga earlier today, and he bought my shit in Chanel without hesitation or without asking for my number. Then, I was just sitting at the bar, and he walked up while some dude was trying to buy me a drink and told the nigga he got it. I was about to ask for his number but I saw a girl walk into the Chanel store and kiss him as I walked out. So, I asked him was he married and he said yes. That just ruined my night lowkey and I'on even know his ass." Gabriel laughed even though she was serious.

"Where he at?" Monique queried, and Gabriel looked across the club where she saw him retreat to and found him staring at her. Goosebumps popped up on her skin and a giddy feeling took over her body.

"Bitch, that's Ray! He's the most important nigga in the city outside of our baby daddy. He got money too. His bitch daddy apart of the cartel."

"That nigga could have had me." Gabriel spoke while staring back at him. She looked away first because it was clear that he wasn't. They were in a trance.

Gabriel, Gina, and Monique were there for two hours when Echo walked in to get Monique.

"You ready Pooh?" Gina was also ready to go but Gabriel wasn't. She was having too much fun.

"Just come with us! Baby mama, you sure you're going to be okay?" Monique asked for the millionth time, and Gabriel said yes even though she was drunk as a skunk.

Monique and Gina left. Gabriel stayed by herself for another twenty minutes then she got up and headed outside. She got behind the wheel of her car. A couple of minutes later, Ray knocked on the window, startling her. She let the window down and he reached in, opening the door.

"Scoot over," he ordered, and she did as she was told.

He quietly drove her to one of his many homes while she dozed off. He admired her beauty without shame as she lightly snored. He got out and unlocked the door to his house before scooping her up and carrying her inside. He laid her in the bed in one of his many guest rooms. He pulled her shoes off and admired the hot pink polish that decorated her toenails. He walked out, leaving her to it.

The next morning, Gabriel awoke, looking around the room. She didn't have a clue where she was and nothing about the room was familiar. She got out of the bed and walked towards the window and was confused at all the woods that surrounded her. She stood at the window, racking her brain, trying to figure out how she got there then that's when it hit her *Ray*. She laughed out loud to herself as she rushed inside the bathroom to get herself together. The last thing she wanted was for him to see her looking crazy. She opened the closet and found a toothbrush, rag, towel, and soap. She brushed her teeth and washed her face before getting in the shower. When she walked out the bathroom, someone was sitting bags of clothes inside the room she was occupying.

"Shit!" Gabriel screeched as she held her towel tightly.

"My apologies, ma'am, we thought you were still sleeping," the woman explained before quickly walking out.

Gabriel locked the door and looked through the bags for something to wear. She stepped into a pair of panties before getting dressed in a mint green Lululemon jacket and the matching pants. The whole outfit looked painted on her body. She grabbed her purse and walked in the bathroom and combed her eyelash extensions out along with her hair. She moistened her face and coated her lips with gloss, making her natural face glow even more than it already was. She put her feet in the Uggs he purchased, and she was ready to go. A knock at the door prompted her to open it. She came face to face with the same lady that had brought her clothes in.

"He wants you to have breakfast with him. Come on and I'll make sure all your belongings are in the car that is going to take you home."

"Okay thank you so much." Gabriel smiled. Thanks to Stprix, she was used to the finer things and being waited on hand and foot but it hit different coming from a nigga that she hadn't even told her name.

The woman led her to where Ray was waiting for her. He had a newspaper spread open in his hands like he would miss something if he didn't pay extra attention to it.

"Good morning, sir. I have your visitor here for breakfast," the woman announced gaining his attention.

He closed the newspaper and sat it on the table, giving Gabriel his undivided attention. The woman walked off, and Gabriel watched until she disappeared. She wasn't sure how she felt about being left alone with Ray.

"Good morning, Gabriel. Have a seat." Ray stood and pulled her chair out for her. Gabriel sat down and his severs walked out and made them both a plate filled to capacity with everything that the chefs had prepared.

"Thanks for making sure I made it in safe." Gabriel decided to be the first one to break their weird silence.

"You make a habit of going out getting drunk and then can't drive yourself home?" He asked. The tone of his words had her on defense.

"I don't. I've just been going through something and last night was my first time out in a while, and I overdid it." She looked across the table and he was staring at her the same way he did yesterday.

"Going through what?" He inquired, and she frowned because he was being nosey with no shame.

"My nigga ain't my nigga nomo," she replied and that was more than enough for him to read between the lines.

"His loss," Ray shrugged, and she blushed.

"What's your name?"

"You know my name. Like I've learned you're Stprix's favorite baby mothe—"

"Was. He has a new favorite now and I'm okay with that." She lied.

"Can I take care of you?" Ray asked, and she frowned in confusion.

"Don't you have a woman?" It was her turn to be in his business.

"I do. I have a wife, but I want you too. You and your sons will never want for shit."

She pondered on what he was saying but it didn't take long at all because thanks to Stprix, her and her kids didn't want for nothing in life. She was the definition of spoiled rotten.

"If you know I'm Stprix's baby mother then you know I don't want for nothing already. Are you asking me to be your side bitch?"

"I hear you. If that's what you want to call it but you would be my woman."

She stabbed at her eggs, putting a forkful into her mouth.

"I don't know you, you don't know me. We can date and see what comes from that. What will your wife have to say about me?"

"She ain't gon' care and okay, we can do that. We don't know each other but I want you in my world. Ever since I saw you yesterday I knew I had to have you but I'll let you get to know me first."

"Why won't she care? If you don't mind me asking."

"She's dying, and she wants me to find somebody before she leaves here," he revealed and watched the look of sadness wash over her face.

"I'm so sorry to hear that. How are you dealing with all of this?" She asked him as he sliced through his steak.

"Honestly, I been staying busy. Trying to keep my mind on the money. How are you getting past your baby daddy moving on, on you?"

"I haven't been doing so good if I'm being honest. I've had a boyfriend in the past, but I was a virgin when I met him. I'm trying to move on the best that I know how to, if that makes sense to you."

"So we going to heal each other?" He smirked, and she smiled. She was open to getting to know him; she just hoped it wasn't a waste of her time.

"I guess so," she agreed without knowing what she was getting herself into.

17

Stprix was with Jaquie and Fox at his home in the den, getting drunk and watching the game.

"You talked to Pooh?" Fox asked, and Stprix shook his head.

"Nah, not really," Stprix revealed because he didn't have a reason to communicate with his baby mothers now that they were no longer romantically involved. They now only discussed grades, doctors' visits, and anything else that pertained to their children's well-being.

"Word around town she been running around with Ray Watkins," Fox informed.

"That nigga that's married to Vivian Gallardo?" Jaquie asked for clarification.

. . .

"You got proof of that? Or muthafuckas just talking?" Stprix asked, and Fox pulled out his phone and sent Stprix the pictures and the video that was sent to him.

"Yeah that's that nigga. He married into their family and got put on. I heard his wife dying though."

Stprix didn't know how he felt about his baby mama and children being wrapped up in the cartel. Technically, they were born into it but he made it his business to stay separate from his mother's dealings. Stprix looked at the pictures of Ray and Gabriel, and they looked like a happy couple. The video showed them holding hands while two men followed closely behind them with shopping bags in hand. Gabriel looked at him like she looked at Stprix and that let him know that she was feeling him.

Signy had all his women moving on, and he didn't like it but he had to deal with it because Signy was where his heart was. He loved her more than he loved himself. He had his fair share of women but none of them made him feel the way she did. He would do anything for her.

"Maybe the shit will blow over," Fox said, and Stprix knew that it wouldn't. Gabriel was everything a man could ask for in a woman. She was literally his girlfriend without the title and even without it, he treated her as such.

"Doubt it. I would've settled down with Pooh if I hadn't of met Signy. Gabriel was a virgin before I met her and outside of that, she a cool person to be around. She take care of home like a muthafucka. As long as that nigga make her happy, then I'm cool with that shit." Stprix

GLITZ

shrugged. Gabriel could be chaotic when need be but for the most part, she was cool and to herself.

"You really love Fat, huh?" Jaquie cracked, causing Fox to laugh. Stprix didn't find nothing funny. He mugged them and they laughed even harder.

"Nigga, don't call her that shit. The fuck wrong with you?" Stprix snapped at Jaquie with that familiar look of murder on his mind. Jaquie and Fox continued to laugh against their better judgment.

"Calm yo' crazy ass down. We know what that mean, Quie. Signy got a fat p—" Fox started but was silenced by Stprix pulling out his gun and cocking it back.

"You quiet now? Nigga you forgetting that I been all in that pussy that you in love with. Nigga, I taught her how to please y—"

Stprix started but Fox hit him with a right hook to the mouth. They sent blow after blow each other's way, neither backing down.

"Aye, chill the fuck out before I shoot y'all stupid muthafuckas!" Jaquie forcefully jumped in between them while taking punches from both sides.

Stprix walked upstairs, and Signy was in the kitchen with Story and Stetson. They were baking cookies. Signy and Stprix shared glances, and she knew something was wrong with him.

. . .

"Watch your sister for me?" Signy took Story who was strapped in a chair on the counter and placed her chair on the floor.

"Okay," Stetson watched as she rushed out the front door behind Stprix.
She pulled on his door handle, and he looked at her. He unlocked the door, and she got in, straddling him.

"What's up? What's wrong?" Signy kissed his neck over and over because she could see the anger dancing in his eyes.

"Nothing," he lied, and she smacked her lips.

"You not leaving this house so get out this car. You got company and everything." She argued unbeknownst to the fight he just had with Fox.

"I'm not trying to leave. I just need a minute to myself."

"Okay." She kissed his lips and got out. She walked in the house and headed back for the kitchen. She washed her hands, and they picked up where they left off.
Stprix walked in the house a few minutes later and went into the kitchen. He slapped hands with Stetson and then kissed Signy. He picked Story up and took her downstairs with him.

. . .

"Crybaby bitch ass nigga," Fox teased as Stprix entered the room.

"Fuck you! Don't speak on my woman, nigga."

"Nigga and don't fucking speak on mine. Or I'ma hit you in yo' shit again." Fox walked up on him and took Story from him.

Jaquie just laughed because his best friends were a trip and extra tender about the women they loved.

* * *

Gabriel was at home in her seven-bedroom mansion, cleaning up when the doorbell rang. Stprix had been by earlier to get her sons, so she knew it wasn't him. She thought about Gina and rushed towards the elevator. She got on and rode it to the first floor. She walked towards the door and looked out and smiled. Ray was standing there. She opened the door, and he didn't smile back. She pulled him inside and wrapped her arms around him, hugging him tight. She led him to the den and pulled him down on the couch.

"You wanna talk about it?"

"Nah. I needed that hug." He tossed his arm over her shoulder as they sat side by side.

For the past month, the two of them had been on several dates and when they weren't dating, they were on the phone like a middle school couple. She had learned all about his wife, Vivian, who was dying from breast cancer.

. . .

"Are you okay?" She asked because that wasn't like him to just pop up unannounced.

"Yeah. What was you doing?"

"Nothing cleaning up my floor of the house. I was just getting started on my room. You wanna come keep me company?"

"If I go to your bedroom, I'ma want to do more than just watch you clean up," he admitted, looking over at her. Sex hadn't been a part of their relationship but they both wanted to act on it.

"That's cool, too." She stood, grabbing his hand. She led him towards the elevator, and they got on and rode it to the fourth floor. She stepped off first, and he followed her with his eyes trained on her ass.

"We can chill and watch movies, and I can make you something to eat," she offered as he kicked off his shoes.

"I ain't really hungry, but I wouldn't mind holding you right now." He walked towards her bed, and she walked up on him and unzipped his jacket and took it off along with his shirt and pants, leaving him in his briefs. She removed her robe, showcasing the red silk gown that stopped in the middle of her thighs.

His hands explored her body, starting with her breasts. He rubbed them slowly then he gripped her ass where he pulled her body against his and rubbed her ass cheeks. He scooped her up and laid her on the bed before getting in behind her. She turned the TV on, and they snuggled up close. He laid behind her with his arms wrapped tightly around her. Thirty minutes later, she found herself getting sleepy.

"You gon' put me to sleep." His grip tightened, and she felt safe with him. She had moved on but she was scared that she wouldn't be enough for Ray. He was losing his wife and at times, she got caught up on being his rebound.

"I'll be here when you wake up," he assured her with kisses to the back of her neck. She blushed like she always did in his presence. She fell asleep and was awakened two hours later by his ringing phone. He answered, and she could hear the caller ask where he was.

"You're with her. I thought I told you to cut her off. My daughter is over here dying and all you can think about is some whore. Maybe if I kill her you'll be obligated to focus more on my daughter."

"You do realize that your daughter is okay with me talking to her? It's what she wants, actually."

"I don't care what she wants, it's disrespectful and not a good look. You heard what I said."

"Don't fucking threaten me," Ray warned in a tone so cold she was a little scared.

. . .

"I'M NOT THREATENING YOU. I'm threatening the woman you're with."

"NIGGA and that's threatening me. If you fuck with her you're going to see a side of me that you don't want to see." Ray got out of the bed, and she couldn't hear any more of the conversation. She turned the lights on and sat up. A few minutes later Ray walked into the bedroom with a scowl on his face.

"ARE YOU OKAY?" She asked him but he ignored her. She sighed as he began pulling his clothes on. "Sorry," Gabriel said slightly feeling bad. She knew it was wrong to be dealing with a married man despite the circumstances. Wrong is wrong right is right.

"YOU HEARD THAT SHIT?" He turned and faced Gabriel.

"IT WAS KIND OF HARD NOT to." She replied and he gave her his back.

"AIN'T nobody going to fuck with you but me and you can't do this. I ain't tryna create more problems within my family right now. I hope you can understand," he spoke with his back to her.

She stood, walking towards him. He sat on the bench in front of her bed. She stepped in between his legs, pulling her gown over her head, leaving her in her birthday suit. She gripped his chin, and he lifted his head. He slowly roamed her body with his anger-filled eyes. She grabbed his hands and put them on her pierced nipples. She put her foot up on the bench, giving him the perfect view of her pink center.

. . .

"How you expect a nigga to leave after this?" He leaned forward, inhaling her scent and she shuddered. His hands made their way down her body.

"Don't leave," she whispered.

He stood and wrapped his arms around her while kissing her lips. She removed his jacket and pants again. Then, she pulled away from him and pushed his briefs down his legs. She took a good look at his ten-inch veiny dick and her mouth watered. Before he could protest, she took him in her mouth, taking his entire dick down her throat. She deep throated him repeatedly until he was shooting his seeds down her throat. She stood and kissed his neck, and he picked her up. She wrapped her arms around his neck while he carried her to the chaise in her room. He laid her on it and spread her legs wide.

He licked his lips in appreciation as he examined her pussy like he was her OB/GYN. He spread her lips and buried his face in her pussy. She moaned loudly as he devoured her. He was eating her like he loved her, and she didn't think they had reached that level yet. *Or had we?* She thought to herself. She couldn't think about it for too long because her stomach tingled as he nibbled and sucked on her clit.

"I'm about to cum!" She moaned out as she grabbed the back of his head and grinded her pussy against his mouth.

"Fuckkkkk!" She moaned even louder than before as her body trembled. However, he didn't stop there, he continued to lick her up and down while her eyes rolled to the back of her head. He didn't give her sensitive clit any mercy, and she lost it.

"This pussy taste good." He let up just to say that before diving right back in.

He flipped her over onto her knees and sucked her pussy from the back, and she came again. He snatched her down on the floor with him. She laid up under him while he laid in between her legs with his palms beside her. He slid his hard dick up and down her soaking wet center. He smacked her clit with the head of his dick over and over while she moaned.

She grabbed it and put it at her opening, and he pushed into her, going balls deep and stretching her virgin tight walls in the process. He looked down at her with his bottom lip tucked in between his teeth and slow stroked her. It had been a long time since both of them had sex, so he wanted to savor the moment and make it last forever. He sucked her nipples into his mouth and bit them. Then he pulled out of her and French kissed her clit before sliding back inside of her. He pinned her legs back behind her head and picked up his pace as he hit her with deep, deliberate strokes.

The sounds of their skin colliding, along with their moans, filled the room. Long gone was the lovemaking; he was fucking the soul out of her. She came for a third time, creaming all on his dick. He was right behind her, burying his seeds deep inside her womb. He collapsed on top of her, pressing his forehead against hers. He barely let her catch her breath before he was rolling over with his back against the chase while he sat on the floor with her in his lap. He placed his hard dick at her opening again, and she sat down on his dick and bounced up and down in his lap. He wrapped his arms around her, holding her tight while she took his soul.

"FUCK! GOT DAMN!" He tucked his bottom lip in his mouth, trying to keep himself from nutting prematurely.

SHE SPUN around and viciously threw her ass back at him while he helplessly sat on the floor. His hands came down, colliding with her skin. She looked back at him and their eyes met. She continued to slam her ass against him while never breaking eye contact, and his face contorted into pleasure. She went even harder as he grabbed her waist and thrust into her, emptying his seeds deep inside her, and she was right behind him, creaming all over his dick.

He kissed all over her ass cheeks, wanting her to know just how much he enjoyed her. They laid wrapped in each other's arms for what seemed like forever.

"I'll get a Plan B tomorrow."

"Don't. If it's meant to be it'll be. Thank you for being my escape when I needed one. You're beautiful and your soul is even more beautiful and that pussy gon' have a nigga feening for it." He kissed all over her chest before getting up and going into the bathroom.

The shower started, and she got up and went into the bathroom across the hall. She brushed her teeth, and took a quick shower. When she walked back into her room, Ray was putting his clothes back on for the second time. Gabriel was sad, she couldn't deny it. She knew what goodbye felt like, and he didn't have to say it because she could feel it.

She wrapped herself in her robe and sat on the bed. Ray pulled her up and hugged her, holding onto her forever.

"Eww, I'm going to miss you," she whined. They hadn't known each other long but they had hit it off.

"I'll be around. Take care of yourself and call me if you need me for anything, you understand?" He asked, and she nodded. He kissed her lips, sticking his tongue in her mouth. Their tongues collided as they kissed hard.

"Go," she demanded as he pulled away from her.

18

Gabriel was having lunch with all her baby daddy's baby mama's. Her and Monique were on one side of the table and Nya, Katelyn, and Signy were on the other side.

"Cheers to us being able to sit here like a family without their being no drama for once," Katelyn spoke, and Monique laughed.

"What's that supposed to mean?" Monique asked with a sly grin on her face.

"It means that you're the drama," Signy spat, and Monique flicked her off. They had been fine after having a conversation after she dropped Stetson off to them one day.

"I'm just saying. Gabriel, me, and Monique have had a conversation. What about me and you, are we good? I know you've started letting Stone and Junior come over, but I just want to make sure there's no issue and if there is one, I would like to fix it."

Gabriel picked up her drink and took a sip from it. The last thing on her mind was Signy and Stprix. She felt like she was in love with another man for the second time in her life.

"We are good, Signy. I owe you an apology. I'm so sorry for what I said about Saint and not taking into consideration what you were going through back then."

"Awww, look at you bitches finally growing up." Katelyn smiled.

"That just means they've moved on," Nya added.

"Thank you so much. I really appreciate that," Signy spoke with a genuine smile on her face.

"We should all go out tonight and leave Stprix with all the kids," Monique suggested.

"I'm not trying to go out. I don't want to do nothing but get in my bed and sulk." Gabriel pouted. She had really been in a funk since Ray had cut her off. It had been almost two months since they had sex. He would send her a message a few times a week but she hadn't seen him.

"About what?" Katelyn frowned her face up in annoyance.

"I don't want to talk about it. I'm kinda embarrassed." Gabriel played with the straw in her cup.

"Don't be, we're sharing here, and when is the first time we all went out together? Oh you're fucking going!" Nya said flatly.

"No judgement zone," Signy added, and Gabriel poured herself another lemon drop.

"I fucked a married man after he cut me off."

"You fucked Ray, bitch, and didn't tell me!" Monique snapped.

"Hoe, didn't you just hear me say I was embarrassed?" Gabriel rolled her eyes.

"I'm confused, what do you mean he cut you off?" Katelyn pried.

"Sooo, I was in Chanel one day a couple of months ago and as I was checking out, this dude walked up and paid for my stuff. He didn't ask for my number or nothing. Boom, I see him in the club later that night. Some dude was trying to buy me a drink, and he was like 'I got it.' We still didn't exchange numbers. I ended up getting drunk as fuck, thinking I could drive home. He walked up on my car and knocked on the window. I let him in, and he drove me to one of his homes."

"The next morning, he tells me he wants me but he has a dying wife, so I was like 'huh?' and he said his wife wants him to have someone before she dies. So we get to kicking it. He took me on a million dates and shopping sprees. He popped up at my house almost two months ago, and we end up falling asleep. His phone rings and it

GLITZ

wakes me up. I can hear his father-in-law on the phone snapping about me and him, telling him that's what his wife wants, and he's basically saying he don't give a damn and that it's disrespectful, and he was like what he need to do, kill me to get him to focus. Ray cut me off but before he left, we had sex, and I haven't seen that nigga since."

"You fucked another nigga that ain't Stprix. I never ever thought I'd see the day." Katelyn placed the back of her hand on Gabriel's forehead.

"I know right, and now I feel dumb as fuck. He's been reaching out but it's not the same."

"Don't. You only live one life, live that shit the way that you want," Signy encouraged, hoping to alleviate some of her worry.

"Ray! Ray! That nigga don't play about his wife. I did hear she was dying from one of my little cousins that knows him. They was saying how ever since they got married, he don't be cheating and out and shit nomo and you saying that ain't true?" Nya asked.

Their server walked up and took their food orders. Then, she walked off and all eyes were on Gabriel.

"I'm not saying that's not true 'cause I could tell he wanted to sleep with me but he never made a move. I'll go out 'cause if not, I'll just sit in the house in my feelings. So, where y'all want to go?" Gabriel gave in, and Monique did a little dance.

"We can go to my daddy's strip club," Signy offered, and they all agreed to meet up later.

* * *

GABRIEL ROAD to the club with Monique, who had picked her up. They walked in and found the other ladies in a section with liquor flowing and ones in the air on the floor.

"We need to get a picture so we can send it to my man," Signy said as Saad walked up. She got him to take their pictures while they did a ton of different poses.

They ordered more ones and requested for more strippers. Signy poured Gabriel and Monique a double shot so they could catch up with the rest of them.

Gabriel stood on the couch, along with Signy and Monique, tossing money in the air to the beat of *Step* by Glorilla.

"I don't want nothing soft, I need a stepper, baby stomp the yard!" Gabriel rapped along to beat while tossing a handful of bills in the air. She was feeling herself. She was dressed in a black lace jumpsuit that had her curves looking curvier. It appeared that she was naked underneath but that was how the jumpsuit was made. She couldn't believe she was out with Signy and having a good time. Signy was actually being a good sport, and Gabriel was feeling bad for the way she treated her.

"You really cool as hell," Gabriel said to Signy.

"Cool as a fan," Signy agreed, and they shared a good laugh.

Ten bottles were sent to their section, and they all look confused.

"Signy, I know damn well you didn't order us more drinks. We already got ten damn bottles," Monique griped.

"It wasn't me. Moët, who ordered these bottles?" Signy asked, and Moet pointed across the club. All of their eyes went to the section across the club where Ray was seated with a group of niggas and about ten strippers entertaining them.

"Bitch, that's yo' man!" Monique raved to Gabriel, who rolled her eyes. The bottles didn't flatter her at all whatsoever. If Ray wanted her attention, he was going to have to do more than that.

"And not. I'on even wanna be in here nomo." Gabriel sat on top of the couch, crossing her legs. Stprix, Fox, and Jaquie walked up, and Katelyn and Signy did the most.

Gabriel picked up her bottle of champagne and poured her a generous amount. Gabriel got up, walked out the section, and headed for the bathroom. She went and relieved her bladder. She walked out the stall, and Ray was standing in the woman's bathroom like he had the right to be there. She ignored him as she walked to the sink and washed her hands. He walked up behind her, wrapping his arms around her waist and making her face him even though she didn't want to.

GLITZ

"I missed you." He kissed the side of her neck.

"I can't tell." She pushed him away and grabbed a couple of paper towels to dry her hands.

"Come on, baby, don't be like that." He stepped in front of her, hugging her and gripping two hands full of her ass.

"I know I shouldn't be feeling some type of way but I do. I think I love you, and I can't have you. That's not fair," she confessed the real reason why she was in her feelings.

"I'm feeling you, too, more than I thought I would. Soon enough you can have me. Be patient for me, and I'ma make up for the time we lost," he promised her. The door swung open, and his grip on her tightened as four men walked in.

"Didn't I tell you to stay the fuck away from her?" One of the men said, and Gabriel recognized the voice from the phone. In fact, she would never forget it.

"Nigga is you fucking crazy? You following me now?" Ray seethed through clenched teeth. He felt like him and his father-in-law had a decent relationship but he was about to ruin it by treating him like he was his son or better yet like a little boy.

"Go on. I'll get up with you later," Ray dismissed Gabriel with his eyes trained on them.

He could tell she was nervous by the way she clung to him. She let him go and moved towards the door, when one of the men grabbed her ass. Ray swung on him, knocking him off his feet. Then, the other two men acted like they wanted to make a move, but Ray put his hand on his hip. The bathroom door opened, and two of Ray's men appeared and so did Stprix, along with Fox and Jaquie. She pushed past everyone until she was in Stprix's arms. Ray's men walked in, standing at his side.

"What the fuck going on?" Stprix looked around the room.

"Let's go!" Gabriel grabbed his arm, pulling him away because she knew her baby daddy and the last thing she needed was for him to make the situation worse.

"G!" Ray called out. She looked back at him. He walked up on her while she was standing beside Stprix. His hands went to her waist

19

Gabriel was home with her baby daddy and Signy. Stprix wasn't letting go of what happened at the club. He wanted to know every detail. She told him everything, and he was livid. He had done a good job of keeping his baby mothers safe, and he didn't want them with someone that couldn't do the same.

"Call that nigga," Stprix demanded, and she shook her head.

"Not tonight, Prix. I just want to lay down. We don't talk anymore, anyway, so it's okay," she tried to reason, and he looked at her like she was crazy.

"Fuck you mean that shit okay when a nigga threatening your life. You ain't gotta call the nigga but you know I'ma get to the bottom of it. Good night." Stprix hugged her and walked outside, leaving Signy behind.

"Call us if you need us," Signy said with a sympathetic look on her face.

"I will, I promise. I had fun tonight. We have to do it again. Send me them pictures of all of us." Gabriel followed Signy to the door.

"Okay." Signy walked out and got in the car with Stprix.

Gabriel locked herself inside her home with her back against the door. She thought about Ray and what he was doing. As if she thought him up, a message popped up from him on her phone.

Ray: I just sent a truck for you. It should be there in ten minutes. Pack a bag

She wanted to tell him no but it was no way she was doing that. She rushed upstairs, packed a bag, and took her heels off. She stepped into a pair of slides. Her phone went off with another text message, letting her know to come out. She walked outside and a black truck was outside with a man standing by the back door that she didn't know. She was leery but she trusted Ray. She got in, and he closed the door before walking around and getting in behind the wheel. Gabriel's phone went off with a text from Signy with the pictures of them. She smiled hard at them; it was like they were best friends when they were just throwing hands not too long ago.

* * *

GABRIEL WALKED onto the gravel in a robe. The night skies were the perfect backdrop as she sauntered towards Ray, who was seated in the jacuzzi with a blunt in his mouth.

"You getting in with me?" He watched as she opened her robe, exposing her birthday suit. She pushed it off and it dropped to the ground. He stood, holding his hand out for her. She grabbed his hand as she climbed into the water.

"I'm sorry about earlier." He stood across from her with one arm around her waist while he smoked with his free hand.

"Sorry for what? At least I know you gon' stand on all ten about me." She blushed, causing him to smirk.

"Fasho."

She backed away from him and sat down, getting comfortable.

"How you been?" He asked, and she shrugged. He cocked his head to the side.

"I've been fine, working and taking care of my sons. How about you? How is your wife doing?" She asked, even though she was scared to intrude. They talked about everything but that was a tough subject for him.

"Shit still the same. I'm still trying to come to terms with this shit," he admitted, and she didn't really know what to say because nothing would really be the right thing.

"It's going to take some time. I'm here if you need me. Have you been taking care of yourself?" She shot him a stern look, and he nodded.

"I was surprised to see you out tonight."

"It was my nigga's birthday, and I promised them niggas I would go. I didn't expect to see you but I'm glad I did."

"Whateverrr. I should stay away from you, you done painted a target on my back." She laughed but little did she know, David Gallardo would kill her about nothing.

"That's the main reason I fell back from you," he revealed what she already knew. When he got up in the middle of the night, she figured as much but he had just confirmed it for her.

"What you said earlier, you meant it?" She asked, and he cocked his head to the side again.

"Stop! You irking!" She splashed water towards him.

"Okay you want to play with that wig on? You know I meant that shit, stop playing with me. I ain't even no cheating type nigga, and then a nigga run across *you*," he shook his head like he was trying to figure out what it was about her that had him doing a three-sixty, especially with his wife on her death bed.

Even though Vivian had given him the green light, he had never stepped out on her and didn't plan to until he met Gabriel. She was his little escape.

"You can fuck my hair up if you pay for it to get fixed, Mr. I Got It. I don't like that you're married or that your wife is dying, but I like you a lot. I can't deny that."

He walked up on her and she held her arms out, halting him.

"You like me or you in love with me?" She allowed him to wrap his arms around her that time.

"What you think?" She asked, and he chuckled.

"I got love for you, too. Things between us are going to get worse before they get better. Don't give up on us, aight?" He said, and she gave him a small smile.

"Okay."

20

Stprix was seated, waiting for his guest to arrive. He had a glass of Hennessy in hand. He tossed it back as Ray Watkins walked into the establishment. Stprix stood to his feet, and they shook hands.

"Should I be worried about your father-in-law?" Stprix got straight to the point. A server walked up, and Ray ordered a double shot of Hennessy.

"I been staying away from her just so it won't be a problem."

"What if that ain't enough? I ain't saying you can't protect her but you got your hands full." Stprix picked up his drink and tossed it back.

. . .

GLITZ

"That would be fucked up of me to get her involved in my bullshit and not make sure she straight. I get it you love your baby mama but I got her now," Ray said as the server brought out his drink.

"I do and you can't be everywhere at once so what does that mean for her?"

Ray picked up his phone and tapped away at the keyboard. A couple minutes later, he passed Stprix his phone. Stprix nodded his head in approval.

"Them the niggas that follow me around daily. She don't know they're following her, and I would like to keep it like that. I got her," he repeated.
    Stprix didn't know how to feel. He was the only man Gabriel had been with and even though he loved Signy, he wanted what was best for all of the mothers of his children.

"Nigga, I hear you but I'm telling you now if they fuck with my baby mama, I'm putting them niggas in the dirt."

"Understood. I might have to discuss some shit with you at a later date just depending on how all this goes down."

Stprix and Ray stood, and Stprix extended his hand to him. They shook hands, and Stprix walked out. His phone rang with a call.

"What, Pooh?"

. . .

"Why you didn't tell me?"

"Cause I didn't have to. You think I'm such a crash out. You didn't even want to arrange the shit, so I had to do it myself." He frowned his face as if she could see.

"I don't think you're a crash out, Alex, I know it. I just didn't want to cause issues for either of you. Everything has been going so good with the family, and I want it to stay that way. Then, his wife is dying, like I don't know what to do or say to that man." She sighed. Stprix got in his truck and brought it to life.

"Just be you, that's more than enough. That man love you. He tryna check me on the low like a muthafucka talking about some *I got her.* That nigga said it twice too," Stprix griped, and Gabriel's laughter filled his ears.

"Thank you, baby daddy."

The phone grew silent so silent Gabriel thought he hung up. Stprix had his way for so long, but now that he had Signy, she was making him see the fault in his ways. He was thankful for his woman.

"I didn't tell you enough but I appreciate you. Sorry I didn't do better by you because you worth it all, remember that shit and don't let no fucking body play with you. Not that nigga you love or his people 'cause I'm smoking shit about you."

. . .

"You didn't have to tell me you been crazy about me for so long, I know how you coming. I'm happy for you. Do right by Signy and even though I don't feel like you drug me along, don't make her feel like that."

Stprix heard her loud and clear. Even though he already had big plans for him and Signy. He loved her. She was his everything, and he couldn't wait to grow old with her.

"I got you. Call me if you need me, okay?"

"Okay," she agreed.

Stprix hung up and headed in the direction toward his home. He pulled into the garage, got out, and went inside. All of his children were on Christmas break. Every break, he kept the kids and on Christmas morning, his children's mothers were there to greet them. However, now he had Signy, and they were switching some things up.

Stprix looked around the house for them and was surprised to find them outside in the back yard. They were all bundled up while they stood around the fire pit, making s'mores. Stprix stood back for the longest, snapping pictures until Stone noticed him.

"Daddy!" Stprix Jr. ran up, hugging him.

. . .

"WHAT'S UP, SON?" Stprix smiled as he wrapped his arms around him. He walked towards them and shook his sons' hands. Then, he squeezed in beside Signy and kissed her lips. Story, who was wrapped in a blanket in her lap, whined for him as she held her arms out for him.

"HEYYY, Daddy Rainbow! I missed you, too!" Stprix laughed as she wrapped her arms around his neck, hugging him.

"SHE'S BEEN CRYING a lot today. I think she's teething," Signy said, watching Story jump up and down in Stprix's lap.

"SHE LOOKS HAPPY NOW. You missed your daddy, Bow?" Stprix rubbed his nose against hers and frowned.

"HOW LONG Y'ALL been out here? My baby face cold as fuck?" He questioned, and Signy knew he was about to get started.

HE GOT up and took Story inside. He knew his sons weren't going to try to come in until they almost had frost bite. Unbeknownst to him, the kids were planning to sleep in the backyard. Stprix took Story's coat off and wrapped her in one of her blankets before cradling her in his arms. She began nodding off, and Stprix walked upstairs to her nursery and sat in her rocking chair. He held onto her for twenty minutes just staring at her sleep.

Story had brought so much happiness into his life. Her and her mother were just what he was missing. The door opened, and Signy appeared in the doorway. He got up and carefully laid Story in her bed. Then, he followed Signy across the hall to their bedroom. He smacked her ass, and she looked back at him.

GLITZ

. . .

"Stop, nigga, I'm cold as fuck," she whined. He walked up on her and unzipped her coat. He stuck his arms in her coat and wrapped his arms around her. They stood like that until Stprix had transferred some of his body heat to her.

"You sleeping in the backyard with us?" Signy asked, and he shook his head. She walked towards the window and motioned for him to come see the tents that they had put up.

"The heat is blowing inside. Me, you, and Story have our own tent and the boys want to sleep together," Signy informed him as he stared, looking unsure.

"If it's not warm enough for me, my baby not sleeping outside, y'all muthafuckas crazy."

Signy rolled her eyes at him but she didn't say anything because it was pointless. He backed Signy towards the bed and pushed her down on it. He laid on top of her and kissed her lips lovingly. She slid her tongue in his mouth and their tongues collided. Signy moaned in his mouth. He pulled away from her and walked out the room. He checked on Story before walking back in his room and locking the door. Signy was in her birthday suit and waiting for him in the middle of the bed.

"You a fucking freak." He laughed, and she shrugged. He removed his clothes and climbed in bed with her. He reached out and grabbed her and she was ice cold.

. . .

"You cold," he complained, and she spread her legs. His eyes were fixated on her second set of lips.

"Warm me up." He laid on top of her and kissed her lips. They were in a intense lip lock when he slid into her. No matter how much they had sex, it felt like the first time every time.

* * *

Signy was at Saint's, working. She felt good being back in her element doing what she loved most. She had a total of ten clients for the day and was on her fourth one. She had Story with her to keep her company. Signy was happy that she had been on her best behavior all day. Her phone rang with a FaceTime call from Stprix. She answered, and sat the phone up where he could see them both.

"Daddy BowBow!" Stprix exclaimed and laughed as Story went crazy in her walker.

"Don't get her turnt up or you're coming to get her," Signy warned.

"You just mad I didn't speak to you first," Stprix teased, and Signy shot him a bird.

"Heyyy, Fat, daddy miss you too," Stprix cooed and watched her blush uncontrollably.

. . .

GLITZ

"What is it, Prix? I'm working." She held her palette in hand with her brush in the other one.

"You want me to come get Rainbow?"

"If you want to."

"Okay. I love y'all." He hung up before she could reply. Signy was obsessed with her man like he was with her. She sometimes randomly laughed at herself because she had a man and not just any man but Stprix Alexander.

"Y'all are so cute," her client raved.

"Thank you, that's my baby. You like it?" Signy passed her a mirror and her client beamed at her reflection.

"I love it! I'm so glad you're back. How much do I owe you?"

"You can give me a hundred since I been MIA." Signy rushed around, cleaning up her mess in preparation for her next client that was due in twenty minutes.

"Thank you! Bye, pretty girl!" The lady passed Signy a hundred dollar bill and a twenty before heading towards the door.

. . .

"Thank you so much, stay warm." Signy walked her out and down the hallway to the top of the stairs that led to the rest of the salon downstairs.

The sound of Story crying caused her to roll her eyes. Thanks to everybody in their lives, Story was spoiled.

She saw Signy walk into the room, and Story really started crying.

"Girlll you spoiled as fuck!" Signy fussed as she washed her hands. She picked Story up, and she instantly stopped crying.

"Momma's girl a crybaby." Signy kissed her lips and placed her on her hip so she could get her some snacks. There was a knock at the door, and Signy opened the door coming face to face with her fifth client.

"Joy?"

"Hey, I'm early. I hope that's okay?" Joy, her new client, asked.

"Yes, that's fine come on in. I'm just getting my baby situated." Signy led her to her chair and put Story back in her chair. Signy put snacks on top of Story's walker and hoped that she would be on her best behavior, especially since Joy was a new client.

"She's beautiful. Thank you."

GLITZ

"Be a good girl for Mommy, stank," Signy pleaded with Story. Signy turned the TV on to Ms. Rachel, and Story watched TV while snacking.

"WHAT KIND of look you going for?"

"IT'S my sister's engagement party so you can do whatever you think would look okay," Joy replied, and Signy got started. Five minutes into her doing her makeup, Story started crying.

"SORRY," Signy apologized to Joy as she picked Story up.
 Signy was kicking herself for not bringing her carrier that she could attach to her body. It took Signy ten minutes to put Story to sleep. She laid her in the bassinet she kept there and started back on Joy. She was almost done when Story began crying again. There was a knock at the door, and Signy opened it coming face to face with a man she had never seen before. She was confused until he greeted Joy.

"GIVE ME LIKE TWO MINUTES. I'm so sorry." Signy walked away from the door, and Joy smacked her lips. Signy thought she was doing that to her but she just had to be tripping. She tended to Story, who was on her way back to sleep.

"IT'S BEEN MORE than two minutes," Joy sassed. Signy turned around and looked at her like she was crazy but she didn't say nothing. Once she was sure Story was really sleeping, she laid her down.

"YOU WANT TO LEAVE OR WHAT?" Signy didn't like her attitude whether she was in the wrong or not. Her child came before whoever.

. . .

"Not until you finish my makeup."

Signy took a deep breath and swallowed her anger that was threatening to show its face.

Signy finished her makeup in three minutes and the silence in the room was smothering. Signy passed her a mirror, and Joy rolled her eyes.

"Is there something you want me to fix?"

"Nope. I'm ready to get the fuck out of here. How much I owe you?"

"One twenty," Signy replied.

"One twenty for this and your damn baby was crying the whole time," Joy complained, and Signy laughed.

"Ohhhh, I see you're one of those." Signy continued to laugh.

"One of what?" The dude asked, interjecting himself in the conversation. The door opened, and Stprix walked in the room, unbeknownst to the drama that was brewing.

. . .

"A BITCH that books my time and finds shit to complain about so she ain't got to pay. I ain't talking to you so don't talk to me," Signy said to the man as Stprix walked towards her, kissing her.

"WHAT THE FUCK GOING ON?" Stprix looked around the room in confusion.

"WHAT YOU MEAN FIND shit to complain about, your damn baby been hollering since I walked in this bitch!" Joy raised her voice.

"CHILL, BAE," the man warned but it was too late.

"SHE'S THE OWNER; she can cry anytime she want to in this bitch! They ain't tryna pay or something?" Stprix asked Signy with his eyes on them.

"WE DIDN'T SAY THAT," the man replied, and Signy just shook her head.

"FAT?" Stprix turned to face her.

"NOPE," she replied, and Stprix hemmed the man up by the collar of his shirt. The man recognized Stprix. When he dropped Joy off, he didn't know that Stprix's woman was doing her makeup.

"YOU GON' let him handle you like that?"

. . .

"Just pay the man!" The man yelled.

"Pay my wife and shut up 'cause I'll handle yo' ass too about mine," Stprix warned.

"Joy!" The man yelled again. She dug in her purse and pulled out the money and threw it at Signy.

Stprix let the man go and grabbed the woman up out the chair by her wig and made her bend over and pick the money up. He didn't have to tell her what to do with it because she eagerly put the money in Signy's hand.

"I want all the money in yo' purse and in yo' pockets, nigga," Stprix demanded as Story began to cry again.

"You still got something to say about my baby crying, bitch?" Stprix asked Joy as she reached into her purse and pulled out all the money inside. She shook her head from side to side and with shaky hands she gave the money to Signy. The man quickly did the same.

"Now get the fuck out!" Stprix snapped, and they scurried out the room like roaches. Signy sat all the money on her workstation and sanitized her hands before picking Story up.

"Stank, what's wrong why you keep crying? You and your damn daddy are troublemakers," Signy cracked.

. . .

GLITZ

"Shid, 'cause she a baby, them stupid muthafuckas tripping." Stprix kissed Story's lips, and she eagerly reached for him. He took her and kissed all over face before she laid her head on his shoulder. He rubbed her back. Signy sat down and counted the money and thanks to her baby daddy, she had come up on three thousand dollars.

"How did the meeting go?" Signy asked.

"Cool, that nigga in love and shit." He shrugged. It wasn't much to say.

"You mad?"

"Why the fuck would I be mad?" He fussed, and she rolled her eyes at him because he had let them get him worked up even though it never took much for Stprix.

"Just saying." She mockingly shrugged, purposely antagonizing him.

"I got this lil' chocolate fine shit with a tight, fat pussy and a deep throat." He pulled her into them, and he kissed her lips repeatedly.

"Is that all I'm good for?"

"Hell naw but that's why a nigga real crazy about you."

. . .

"You make me sick. Take your daughter with you 'cause y'all messy, and I don't have time to be at my place of business tussling with bitches, and you sir have no sense, but I love you so damn much," Signy said, causing him to blush.

"I love you too, Fat."

Signy walked around the room, packing up all Story's stuff. Then, she took her from Stprix and made sure she was still dry before putting her coat on and zipping her up. She passed Story to Stprix and then picked up the diaper bag and gave it to him.

"Damn, Bow you see yo' mammy really tryna put you out."

"Nigga, don't tell my baby that." Signy kissed Story's lips and then Stprix's before walking them out.
 Signy loved her little family. She thanked God for them every day because she didn't know what she would do without them. She stood in the door, watching Stprix strap her into her seat. He turned around, blowing her a kiss and she caught it, holding it close to her chest. He smirked before walking around to the driver side.

21

Gabriel was at home eating breakfast with her children. They were all gathered around the table. Gabriel scrolled through her Instagram feed while her boys watched the TV that Stprix was adamant that she have in the dining room. Her mouth opened and closed in shock after what she just read. Then, her mind went to Ray. She continued to scroll and his wife's face was all over her timeline. She passed at thirty-five years old. Her morning had been ruined by that information because she could only imagine how he must have felt. She didn't feel like he deserved the hand he was dealt but that was life for you.

"What's wrong, Ma?" Stone asked after looking at her face.

"Nothing, baby. What y'all want to do today?"

"Can we go to the arcade?" Junior asked, and she nodded.

"Yeah we can just let me know when y'all ready to leave. Make sure y'all's rooms clean." Gabriel got up and washed her hands at the sink before going upstairs to her room.

She undressed and got in the shower. She got out and put a robe on before sitting at her vanity. She moisturized her face and did a light beat. Then, she pulled her bonnet off and ran her hands through her natural tresses that hung to her ass. She brushed her curly hair out and brushed it up into a high ponytail on top of her head. She placed a pair of diamond hoops in her ears. After she was satisfied with her look, she went in the closet and got dressed in a army green sweatshirt with the matching pants. She put on a pair of thick socks before stepping into her Ugg slides. She put on a matching puffer vest to complete her look. Stone and Junior walked in the room, and they were ready to go, too.

"Y'all rooms clean?"

"Yes ma'am," they answered in unison. She grabbed her purse and walked out the door. She went to check their rooms while they went downstairs. Once she was sure their rooms were clean, she found them in the garage inside her Maybach. She got in and drove them to the arcade they frequented often.

They walked inside, pulled out their cards, and took off. Gabriel found a table where she could see them, unbeknownst to her she had men watching her every move. She pulled her laptop out of her purse and caught up on her work.

"Hey, Gabby!" Their normal sever, Julian, greeted her.

"Hey, girl! What's up?"

"Nothing much. it's been slow in here today. I came over to see if you wanted to order something."

"Not yet but probably so in a hour." Gabriel knew her sons after running around for a couple of hours, they would want pizza wings and Italian ices.

"Okay, I'll be back." Julian walked away, and Gabriel looked around the arcade, laying eyes on her sons.

Almost two hours later, Junior ran up. He kissed Gabriel's cheek and she blushed.

"I'm hungry and thirsty."

"Go find Julian and place an order, Get me a salad too," she yelled as he rushed off.

Her mind went to Ray. She wanted to reach out to him but she didn't know what to say. She pulled out her phone and went to their text thread. She hadn't talked to him in two days. After their weekend at his penthouse, he consistently stayed connected with her. The night he made love to her in the jacuzzi constantly played back in her head like a rated R movie.

She sent him a text message after contemplating what to say for fifteen minutes. Then, she placed her phone down. Julian brought their food out and her kids were right behind her, causing Gabriel to laugh at them. They were eating and talking when Ray walked up. Gabriel's eyes lit up at the sight of him.

"I'll be right back," she said to her boys.

She grabbed Ray's hand and led him to the hall to give them privacy. She stood on her tippy toes and wrapped her arms around his neck. He wrapped his arms around her waist. She didn't have to say anything because her hug was soothing enough.

"I need you."

"I'm here. Whatever you want?" Gabriel gripped his cheeks, staring into his bloodshot red eyes.

"I'm about to go out of town for a week. Can you come?"

"Yeah. I just need to check with Stpr—"

"For what?" He twisted his handsome face up in annoyance.

"To see if he can watch the boys. He will, though. When we leaving? I look a mess."

"No you don't. You got time to do whatever you need but I like your hair the way it is." He pecked her lips and walked away. He left her standing there with a lot to digest.

***

GABRIEL AND RAY were staying at a private villa in the Dominican. It was their second day and she agreed to come, but he had been in his own room. She barely saw him. She sat on the beach on a daybed, eating breakfast with a glass of champagne. She finished eating then went inside after cleaning the sand off her feet. She made Ray a plate of food that his chef prepared. She walked to his side of the villa and without knocking, she walked into his room to the sounds of crying.

Gabriel froze in her tracks. She swallowed deeply before continuing her stride. He was under the covers, unbeknownst to her presence. She sat the food on the nightstand and braced herself. She pulled the covers back and was greeted by his tear-stricken face. She climbed in the bed, laying her body on top of him. They wrapped their arms around each other. Gabriel found herself shedding tears with him.

"It's going to be okay, baby," she whispered.

"This shit hurt bad," he struggled to get out.

"I know." She tightened her grip on him, wishing she could take his pain away. He cried himself to sleep. Gabriel got up and went to get a wet rag. She gently wiped his face, careful not to awake him.

She got in the bed with him and snuggled up close to him. Three hours later, she awoke to the sound of music playing. She felt around the bed for him and sat up when she realized it was empty. She got up and walked out the room. She discovered Ray in the living room on the couch with a bottle of patron in his hand.

"Baby, come here," he demanded, and she walked toward him, sitting in his lap.

"Did you eat something?"

"Nah. You tryna get drunk with me?" He rubbed her back.

"Yeah let me go find us something to eat. I'll be back." She took the bottle of liquor with her because it was clear he had drank more than enough on an empty stomach. She found the chef in the kitchen, standing at the stove cooking.

"I tried to get him to eat, hopefully you can," Tisha said with sympathy. She fixed both of them a plate and put their plates on a tray.

"I'ma try, thank you." Gabriel smiled and Tisha nodded.

"I'll bring y'all something to drink in a minute."

Gabriel took the tray and carried it back to the living room. Ray wiped his face with the back of his hand, not wanting Gabriel to see that side of him again.

"Baby, it's okay to cry or feel how you want to feel, but you have to take care of yourself." She picked up his plate of steak, potatoes, and broccolini and cut up his steak. She stuck the fork in the steak and potatoes and held it up to his mouth. He opened his mouth with his eyes trained on hers. She silently fed him until his plate was empty.

GLITZ

"You want some more?" She asked, picking her plate up and he nodded. "When the last time you ate and don't lie," she quizzed as Tisha walked in with their drinks. Gabriel thanked her and she left.

"When we left," he admitted, and she sighed but didn't say anything because she understood.

She put a piece of steak in his mouth before feeding herself. She took turns feeding him and herself until her plate was gone.

"Now can I get drunk in peace?" He asked sarcastically, and she smirked.

"Yeah." She picked up the bottle and passed it to him. He turned it up, filling his mouth. Then, he grabbed her by the throat and spit the liquor into her mouth.

"Now you tryna start shit." She groaned.

"I can finish whatever I start." He turned the bottle up again and took a generous swig before passing it to her. They got drunk together and then went back to his room and had sex all night.

The next morning, Gabriel awoke to an empty bed. She got up and limped into the bathroom. Her pussy was sore and so was the rest of her body. She relieved her bladder before washing her hands at the sink. Then she brushed her teeth, and washed her face. Ray walked in the bathroom, and she walked towards the closet.

"Why you limping?" He stared at the bruises on the back of her neck, back, and ass cheeks.

"Why you think?"

"My bad." He walked up behind her and kissed her bruises even the ones on her ass.

"I enjoyed it." She quickly let him know he had nothing to be sorry for.

He walked towards the tub that sat in front of a window with an ocean view and filled it with hot water. Once it was full, he led her to the tub and held her hand while she climbed in.

"I'ma let you soak for a minute, then I'ma come back and wash you up." He kissed the top of her head.

"Okay." She blushed.

He closed the door and she settled in the water and enjoyed the view. Her mind ran rampant as she overly thought about the future. She had a bad habit of that, and she was trying to work on it especially if she was starting something new with someone else.

Thirty minutes later, the door opened, and Ray walked in the bathroom kneeling beside the tub. He let the water out and let the water run while he began washing her up. She closed her eyes, loving every second of it. Once she was clean, he helped her out.

"I know it's not the time for this, but I love you," she confessed as he wrapped a towel around her.

"How come it ain't? I need all the love you can give a nigga," he stated truthfully, and she blushed like she always did in his presence.

"I love you, too, and my baby." He placed his hand on her stomach, and her eyes went to his hand in confusion. She wasn't pregnant or at least she didn't think she was.

"You're pregnant," he told her instead of asking her, after seeing the look of confusion wash over her.

She walked in the room, picked up her phone, and went to the app that tracked her period. She sat down on the bed after realizing she was almost two weeks late.

"What the fuck?" She whispered aloud to herself. He sat down beside her and she faced him.

"How do you know?"

"My grandmother is a psychic. She called and woke me up this morning going on and on about it," he revealed.

"That doesn't mean anything," Gabriel said in denial even though her period had never been that late.

"She has never been wrong about anything. We can go find a doctor's office if you want to." For the longest, they sat in silence thinking extremely hard.

"Are you even happy about this?" She questioned, and he frowned deeply.

"Of course, I am, baby. I need you and my daughter. Finding that out made me feel like everything is going to be okay. I lost my best friend but I gained you and my first child." He leaned towards her and kissed her lips.

GLITZ

"She said it's a girl too?!" She exclaimed, and he laughed while nodding his head.

"What if she's wrong for the first time?"

"Then, we gon' keep trying until you bless me with our first daughter." He shrugged.

She got up and walked out the door. She went into her room and got dressed. She was eager to go to the doctor, and she couldn't wait until they got home. She needed to know now.

* * *

GABRIEL AND RAY were walking through the DR streets holding hands. They had just left the doctor's office and were on cloud nine. Gabriel was indeed pregnant and somewhat in denial. She wasn't shocked that she was pregnant, after all they hadn't used a condom once and he never pulled out. It was only a matter of time before he planted his seeds.

"I want to meet your lil' granny," she said, causing him to chuckle.

"I'll fly you out there before it's too late for you to be flying."

"This is crazy, bae!"

He brought her hand up to his mouth and kissed the back of it. His mind drifted to his deceased wife and a part of him felt bad for moving on so fast even though it was what she wanted.

"You thinking about her?"

"Yeah. Even though she wanted me to have someone else, it feels like I'm betraying her."

"I don't know what to say to that, but I'm sure if she wanted you to move on she's happy for you. Don't ever feel bad for going through the motions of grieving. I'm here, and I got you through whatever."

He stopped walking and turned to face her. He still held her hands in his.

"Thank you, baby." He felt the genuine love she had for him, and he needed it now more than ever. He had lost Vivian but he refused to lose Gabriel. Goosebumps formed on his skin and he looked around, checking his surroundings. He was psychic himself in his own kind of way. He spotted one of his father-in-law's men.

Then bullets rang out in their direction. He pushed Gabriel into one of the shops that they were standing in front of. He led her to the back of the shop with his men following closely behind them with their guns in hand. Gabriel freaked out at the sight of them.

"Chill, they are with us. Are you okay?" He examined her from head to toe. His men went out the back door and checked the alley.

"Come on, Boss Man, nobody's in the alley." One of his men poked their head inside. Ray put his hand on the small of her back and led her outside to a truck that was waiting for them. He got in behind her and his driver pulled off. They got back to their villa and packed up their stuff. Then, he called his pilot and they made their escape.

22

Gabriel was locked in one of Ray's safe houses. He ushered her to the doctor when they returned to make sure everything was okay with their child, and she learned that she was ten weeks pregnant with a daughter. She was happier than ever but she worried about the safety of Ray and herself. Her phone rang with a call from Stprix as Ray entered the room. She silenced the call, and he called right back. Stprix had been on one himself after learning about what happened in DR. He kept her sons, refusing to let them out of his sight.

"Who is that?" Ray asked after her phone rang for the third time.

"It's my baby daddy."

"See what that nigga wants." He mugged her.

"He wants to talk to you," she revealed before she answered the phone for Stprix, who demanded to speak with Ray. The funeral was in two days, and she was worried about something happening to her man.

* * *

THE SURROGATE FOR A BILLIONAIRE THUG 2

STPRIX AND RAY were seated in the living room of Ray's safe house. They both wanted David Gallardo in the dirt.

"How you want this shit to play out?" Stprix asked him. They had been drinking and plotting for the last two hours.

"After the funeral that nigga gotta go ASAP."

"Say less," Stprix said as Gabriel stuck her head inside.

"Y'all okay?"

"You nosey, Pooh," Stprix replied, and Ray laughed. She shot him a bird.

"We good, baby," Ray assured her. She walked off, leaving them alone again.

"I'ma get out y'all lil' love nest. I'll be in touch." Stprix stood.

"Don't hate, nigga." Ray smirked. He stood and walked Stprix out. They slapped hands, and Stprix left after getting in his truck.

He headed towards his home. He parked in the garage and got out. He walked in the house and the house was quiet. He went to the kitchen to see what chef prepared. He quickly washed his hands and warmed up his plate.

"Hey, when did you get here?" Signy asked, walking in the kitchen. She walked up on him, and he picked her up. She wrapped her legs around his waist.

"I just got here. Where my baby?"

"I think she sleep."

"I missed you," he said like he hadn't seen her in days. He kissed her lips as he sat her on the counter.

He got his food from the microwave and stood across from her, leaning on the counter while he ate. Once he was done, they went upstairs and she got in the bed while he went in the bathroom to shower. Ten minutes later, he walked out with a towel around his waist. He dried off and got dressed in a pair of briefs and sweats. He pulled a T-shirt over his head and headed for the door. He headed for Stone and Junior's room first then he went to Millenia's room and knocked on the door.

"Come in," she called out, and he turned the knob. She was in the bed and Story was beside her. Stprix smiled at the sight of them.

GLITZ

"You can't have her tonight, Alon."

"Ma, you know I can't sleep without my baby," Stprix argued.

"Trust me I know, but I need her tonight, please let me have that?" She locked eyes with him, feeling like she was staring at herself. They were literally the same person. Stprix was thankful she had stuck around. He had Signy, Story, and Millenia. He felt like he was on top of the world.

"Aight, you good?"

"Yes, son. I'm fine. I love you."

"I love you, more. Thank you for being here," he said, and she wrapped her arms around him. She kissed all over his face, and he ate it up just like Story did when he did it to her.

"Thank you for having me. I'm never leaving."

"You promise?" Stprix asked, and she laughed. When she realized he was serious, she nodded her head.

"I promise, Alon. I'm here. I'm not going anywhere." She was grateful he had given her a second chance.

He walked out of her room and headed upstairs to his room. Signy was sleeping. He took off his clothes and got in bed with her. He snuggled up behind her and began kissing all over her back.

"Where Story?"

"She asked if she could sleep with her. I told her it was cool but if you want me to go get her, I will," Stprix said as Signy went under the cover.

She removed his dick from his briefs and took him into her mouth. They made love for an hour before falling asleep in each other's arms. Stprix got up the next morning and looked over at Signy, who was sleeping. Her nipples were playing peek-a-boo and her bonnet had come off, leaving her hair sprawled all over her head. He could stay and watch her sleep forever but he had something that he had to take care of. He pulled the cover up over her chest and kissed her lips. One of his favorite things to do was wake up to his woman.

He tossed the covers off him and went in the bathroom to handle his hygiene. He walked in the closet and got dressed in black from head to toe. His phone rang letting him know his surprise had arrived.

He walked downstairs to the front door and allowed the workers from the florist shop in. He led them to his bedroom. After they covered the floors in a exaggerated amount of rose petals, they walked in with floating red heart-shaped foil balloons that filled the room. Stprix looked around in approval, glad that they could make his vision come together on such short notice. He walked them out and thanked the four workers with a hundred dollar tip a piece. Then, he headed back upstairs to his room. He walked around to Signy's side of the bed and kneeled beside her. He pulled a box out of his pocket and opened it. Inside was a thirty-carat heart shaped ring.

"Fat?" Stprix called out while gently shaking her awake. She laid on her side, facing him. It took her a minute to grasp what was going on around her but once she did, she sat up with the sheet covering her naked body.

"I love you more than anything in this world. I'm glad you gave me Saint because that was the beginning of our love story. You got me on one knee doing some shit I never thought I would do, but I'll do anything for you. Signy, will you marry me?"

She jumped out of the bed and knocked him over. She hugged him, wrapping her arms around his neck. They laid in the mountain of rose petals.

"Is that a yes, Fat?"

"Yessss, nigga you know that!" She kissed his lips, and he smiled.

"When we getting married?" He asked, and she shrugged.

"We can do it right now if you want to," she offered.

"Hell yeah, pick the place, and I'll call the pilot, but first I have something I need to take care of. Can you wait for me?" He stood and helped her up.

"Of course, I can," she said as he kneeled in front of her once more. He grabbed her hand and put the huge rock on her finger.

"I can't believe you, you did yo' biggest one everrr!" She put her hands on his shoulders and stared into his eyes. Their love had been through hell and back, and they were still standing.

23

Stprix stood in the shadows awaiting his victim. For the past two days, he had studied everything he needed to know about his prey and now it was time to make a move. Thanks to some intel he had an easy way inside. It was cramped but he didn't have to stay for long. He checked the time on his watch expecting his victim at any minute. The same tunnels that David Gallardo had built in case someone came for him was where his murder would go down.

DAVID WALKED *in his bar after a long day. He had buried his one and only child and it hurt him to the core. His wife died giving birth to her and he'd never tried for another one. Vivian was his world and all he had left in the world that he cared about. He grabbed his most expensive bottle of liquor, opened it, and drank straight from the bottle. His phone rang with a call from his number two, his right-hand man, Jacob.*

"HE'S WITH HER. The Black bitch in Texas, it's the perfect time to kill them both," Jacob greeted.

. . .

"Not right now. I want to be the one to do it." David turned the bottle up and slammed it down.

"This may be the perfect time. His men aren't around."

"Take care of them both." David hung up.

Ray landed on his radar after learning about all the weight he was moving. He offered him his seat in exchange he marry his daughter. Ray and David had a great relationship and so did Vivian and him. She was against marrying a stranger but they hit it off, falling in love instantly. They were together for two years when she was diagnosed with stage four cancer.

David was aware that she had given Ray the green light to date but he didn't think it was right. He'd observed Ray with Gabriel, and he saw the love they shared and it angered him. Ray had stepped down from his business to sit by Vivian's side every day and night. He couldn't take away the fact that Ray was a good husband but he lacked loyalty, and David refused to let his betrayal slide.

David pulled up his surveillance footage and panicked at the sight of the black van in his yard. He jumped up and grabbed his shotgun. He was kicking himself for not allowing his men to accompany him like they always did, but he a wanted to be alone to properly mourn his child. He heard a loud explosion and with his gun in hand, he headed in the direction of the tunnels. His phone rang with a call from Jacob. He answered with his head on a swivel.

"You can't kill me, Pops, but you about to die." Ray laughed in his ear before ending the call. David was kicking his own ass for bringing him into his life.

GLITZ

. . .

DAVID WOULD DEAL with Ray later. He made it up to the bookshelf. He quickly put his code in, and impatiently waited for it to open. Once it did he stepped inside. He breathed a sigh of relief once he was safe and sound. He walked until he was at the utility hole of his tunnels. He climbed in and looked around checking his surroundings. He couldn't really see because it was so dark.

STPRIX HAD a pair of night vision glasses on, as he stood up against the wall as David Gallardo foolishly walked into his trap. He never minded committing murder when it came down to his family. Gabriel was the mother of his sons, so she was off limits and so were his other four children's mothers He stepped out in front of David and laughed sinisterly as his eyes grew wide in fear. He was staring down his angel of death, and Stprix was eager to send him to meet his maker.

"IT LOOKS like you fucked up, huh." Stprix pulled the trigger, putting a bullet in between his eyes. He collided with the ground, and Stprix left the same way he came in.

* * *

"BABY we really about to do this, fareal?" Signy asked as they stood at the altar in Las Vegas. They had ditched everyone and left Story with Katrina just so they could tie the knot.

THEY STOOD across from each other in disbelief, well Signy was definitely in denial. She always saw herself marrying a woman not Stprix.

"Y'ALL READY?" The man asked, and they both nodded.

. . .

THEY TUNED HIM OUT, staring deeply into each other's eyes as the man began the ceremony until it was time to say their vows.

"FAT, baby girl, my heart, my soulmate, my princesses momma, I love you more than anything in this world. You're my everything and everything a nigga could ask for. You're literally perfect. I know I fucked up our trust before, but I'm never doing that again. I knew when I met you, I wanted to spend the rest of my life with you and I'm thankful that you gave me a chance. We been through hell and back but I promise you nothing but love and sunshine from this moment forward." A couple of tears slid down his face, and her eyes were wet with tears. She wiped his tears away and prematurely kissed his lips.

"AWW, baby, I love you so, so, so much. I didn't see this for me, but I can't be without you. I'll do whatever for you. You make me so happy and you introduced me to a life that I didn't know I needed and want so bad. I can't wait to spend forever with you. Thank you for loving me the way you do."

ONCE THEY WERE OFFICIALLY WED, Stprix gripped her face with both hands and kissed her passionately. They thanked the priest and walked out hand in hand.

"YOU'RE REALLY MY HUSBAND, now that's crazy," Signy smiled, still in shock. He had just made her the happiest woman on the planet. He proposed that morning, and they had just wed at ten that same night.

. . .

GLITZ

"Til death do us apart, you heard that nigga," he said, causing her to laugh.

"Where we going?"

"You'll see." He led her outside to the awaiting black truck that had streamers and cans hanging from the back. He opened the door and white rose petals decorated the floors and seats. A bottle of champagne chilled on ice. He helped her inside and climbed in behind her. There driver pulled off while Stprix popped a bottle of champagne. He poured them both a glass.

"To us!" Signy beamed as they tapped glasses. She was on a high and didn't want to come down. A few minutes later, they arrived at *The Top of the World.*

They walked inside, went upstairs, and walked in the restaurant. Their entire family was there, kids included. Stprix had the restaurant shut down for their reception. Katrina walked up with Saad, who was holding Story. She saw Stprix and went crazy trying to get to him. Stprix took her and kissed her lips, and she wrapped her tiny arms around his neck.

"So you don't see your momma, Stank?" Signy pouted, standing in front of them. Stprix pulled her into them, and wrapped his arm around her waist.

. . .

"Give your momma a kiss, Bow," Stprix said, and Story leaned towards Signy who met her halfway. She gave Signy a wet kiss then she laughed.

"Thank you, Stank!" Signy cooed, rubbing her cheek.

The photographer snapped pictures of them. Stox walked up on them, and Story reached for him next.

"Congratulations, Pops and Ma," Stox greeted, and Signy smiled because she was now officially a stepmother. They had nine kids and counting because she knew Stprix was not done.

"Thank you, baby!" Signy spoke first.

"Appreciate it, lil' nigga," Stprix was next, and Signy just shook her head at him.

They greeted their guest which consisted of only their family members before sitting down and eating. Once they were done, they turned up until two o'clock in the morning before retiring to Stprix's Vegas home.

"How many houses do you own, Mr. Alexander?" Signy asked as he followed her upstairs. She didn't know where she was going but that didn't stop her from venturing further into the house.

. . .

"We own twelve houses, Mrs. Alexander. I use to stay here a lot a few years back. We can stay here a couple of days and go somewhere else if you want or we can stay in and make baby number ten." He walked towards the double doors of the master suite and pushed the doors open.

There were white rose petals in the foyer. She stepped inside with a huge smile on her face. The room was filled to capacity with white floating balloons. A bunch of vases were spread throughout the room that were filled with white roses. It looked like a remake of her proposal but better.

"We can stay in and make baby number ten." She turned to him with the biggest smile. She couldn't stop smiling. Stprix had completely blown her away.

"Get naked. What the fuck you waiting on?" He demanded, and she pulled the white thigh-length Balenciaga dress over her head while he watched. She was left in her black bra, thong, and heels. Next to go was her black lace bra. Stprix licked his lips, eager to get her nipples in his mouth. Then, she turned around and bent over while pulling her thong over ass. He walked up on her, no longer able to keep his hands to himself. They made love all over the room until they tapped out.

EPILOGUE

Katelyn walked in the house after a long day of work. She was still a NICU nurse six years later. She loved her job and probably wouldn't retire until she was old and gray. She walked in the laundry room and undressed then loaded her scrubs inside the washing machine. She started the washer and washed her hands before venturing through her home, looking for her family.

"Mommy!" Kenya yelled when she walked into her play room where her and Fox were chilling.

"Hey, baby! I missed you!" Katelyn picked her up and kissed all over her face. Kenya was her and Fox's five-year-old daughter.

"What I say about picking her up, Katelyn?" Fox snapped.

"I missed you too but I'm about to leave. Zuri coming to get me." She said referring to her big sister.

"Aww, I'm going to miss you. Be good, okay?"

Kenya nodded her little head, and Katelyn placed her back on her feet. Fox greeted her with a much needed hug and kiss after a long day's work.

"Daddy missed you too but quit being so got damn hard headed," he whispered in her ear.

GLITZ

"You and your daughter spoiled as fuck. What you want for dinner tonight?"

"Whatever you feel like cooking but you know what I really want to eat." He kissed her collarbone.

"What, daddy?" Kenya asked, oblivious to the double meaning of their conversation. Katelyn laughed while Fox frowned.

"I'm talking to your momma, go play with your Barbies. I thought you said they was finna go swimming."

"Oh yeah! I almost forgot!" She took off and picked her Barbies back up.

Katelyn walked out the room, and Fox was right behind her. She went to the kitchen so she could start on dinner. Every night, she cooked for her husband and daughter. Stox, who was twenty, moved out two years ago and so did Storm.

As if she thought him up, Stox entered the kitchen and she heard little footsteps behind him.

"Hey, son! You got my baby with you?" The island was blocking her view. She walked around to Stox's side and smiled bright at the sight of her granddaughter, Sagari.

"Heyyyy, granny girl!" Katelyn picked up her one and only grandchild and kissed all over her face like she had just done Kenya.

"Katelyn," Fox warned.

"Hey, GG!" She spoke clear as day. She was three years old and Stox's only child.

"What's up, son?" Fox spoke to Stox.

"Shit, Pops. That stupid bitch talking about some she going out. I got something I need to take care of." Stox frowned, looking just like Stprix.

"Watch your mouth, Stox, especially in front of my baby while you're talking about her momma. What you got to do that's so important that you can't watch your daughter?" Katelyn snapped. Fox took Sagari from her and took her to play with Kenya.

"I always have my child, Momma, you know that. I have a business meeting that I can't miss and it ain't like she can come in the club with me."

Katelyn stared at her oldest son. She was proud of the young man he had grown to be.

"I thought your daddy told you he didn't want you to take over for Millenia? You're getting more and more involved, I see. I'll keep my granddaughter but you need to be careful, baby. I know you and what you're capable of but trust nothing and shoot first and ask questions later. You hear me?"

"I hear you, Ma, and I'm grown. My daddy can't tell me what to do. I've already taken over. I'm the head of the Alexander Dynasty, let me tell him on my own time. I'll be back to get my baby when I'm done. I love you." He kissed Katelyn's cheek and left the kitchen to go see Kenya and tell Sagari bye. He poked his head back in the kitchen on his way out to find Katelyn cooking.

"I love you. I'll drop her off in the morning, so you can go straight in. Be careful."

"I love you more, Ma. Thank you," he said, and she nodded with a smile.

She continued cooking and a hour later, she was plating everyone's food. Fox walked in the kitchen standing behind her. He wrapped his arms around her waist and kissed the side of her neck over and over until she was lightly moaning.

"Why you in here starting shit knowing we babysitting?"

"They gon' eventually go to sleep and that ass is mine." He placed his hands on her stomach and felt his son kick.

"You so nasty, but I'm always horny. I can't wait." She turned, kissing his lips. They were six months pregnant and happy as ever. They both started over because their kids were grown but they were happy nonetheless.

* * *

MONIQUE PULLED into the parking lot of Echo's bowling alley.

"Hurry, Mommy!" Her son yelled from the backseat, causing her to snicker.

Echo opened Monique's door and his mini went crazy.

GLITZ

"Daddyyy!" Little Echo squeaked. He was four going on forty years old.

Echo kissed Monique's lips before opening the back door.

"What's up, twin?" Echo greeted him.

"Get me out, Daddy!" Little Echo demanded, and Echo did what he was told. His four-year-old often bossed him around.

Echo grabbed Monique's hand, and they walked inside the bowling alley. It was semi-packed but the real crowd wouldn't be there until after hours.

"Look, baby, there go Stetson," Monique raved, and Little Echo turned his head in the direction of his favorite person.

"Put me down, Daddy!"

"Nigga say please," Echo demanded.

"Please, Daddy! I wanna see my brother!" Little Echo kissed his lips, and Echo put him down.

"That boy a trip." Echo watched as he ran up on Stetson, who was bowling with his girlfriend. They slapped hands, causing Monique to smile. She loved her sons' bond; they were really close.

"Who you telling? He was doing everything today while I was tryna vlog and shop. I won't be doing that again for a while." Monique thought about how many times she had to get on to him about doing something today and sighed. She was thankful for her love child but he was a piece of work.

"You should've brought him here. I been here most of the day. Stetson just got here like two hours ago. You hungry?"

"Yep, and I want a drink. You know what I want to eat. I'm going to the bar." She took a detour to the bar and ordered a lemon drop.

"Can I get you anything else, Boss Lady?" Linny asked as she sat her drink down on a napkin.

"No thank you, baby." Monique passed her a fifty, grabbed her drink, and walked towards her children.

"Wassup, Momma," Stetson greeted her with a hug and kiss to the cheek.

"Hey, son! You okay? Hey, Strawberry! How are you?" Monique

greeted her son's girlfriend of the last three years. She was holding Little Echo, who was playing with her phone.

"Hey, Momma! I'm good. You look pretty," Strawberry spoke back.

"Thank you, pudding, so do you. I'm about to go find Echo. Do y'all want me to take him?" Monique looked between Stetson and Strawberry.

"E, you want to go with Momma or stay with me?"

Little Echo looked up from Strawberry's phone and looked at Stetson.

"I wanna stay with you, brother," Little Echo replied, and Monique rolled her eyes. Stetson held his fist out, and Little Echo put his fist against his.

"I don't care, lil' boy," Monique playfully pushed Little Echo, who laughed. She walked off and headed to the restaurant in the building that was located on the second floor. She found Echo at a table awaiting her. He stood, and she kissed his lips.

They sat down and five minutes later, their food was brought out.

"This so random but I'm proud of you. You retired and all of your businesses are doing so well," Monique praised her man.

"I appreciate that, Ma, thank you. I'm proud of you, too. You have five nail shops and them bitches stay busy. I almost forgot about your nail polish line. On top of taking care of me and the kids flawlessly. A nigga love and appreciate you." He stretched his arm across the table, and she placed her hand in his.

"Awww, bae, thank you. I love you more." She was so thankful she gave Echo a chance.

Big Emery, her father-in-law, was Stprix's mentor. Stprix had been on his own for so long until Big Emery took to him. Their bond was the reason Echo was still alive after shooting him and the fact that he was just a teenager at the time. Monique used to often worry that her children's fathers wouldn't be able to coexist but they had been, and she was grateful. After all, her and Echo were married and had been for the past three years. He wasn't going nowhere.

* * *

GLITZ

"G!" Ray called out.

"I'm in my makeup room!" She yelled back. He walked in, holding their one-year-old daughter, Remi.

"Where you think you going?" Ray asked as he watched her put the finishing touches on her makeup.

"Out. What you want?"

"You," he replied, and she rolled her eyes.

She finished her makeup in silence then got up. She took Remi from him and walked in the closet. She put Remi down and scanned her many rows of clothes. Ray had just as much money as Stprix, so her life had been upgraded even more. He was still the leader of the cartel.

She decided on a white tennis skirt and a white cropped collar shirt. She stepped into a pair of white open-toe sandal heels. Then she put a diamond studded Cuban link around her neck and secured her diamond studded AP on her wrist.

"Remi, get yo butt over here!" Gabriel fussed while Remi pulled clothes off hangers. She looked at her wedding ring and smiled. She had been married to Ray for five years.

"Aww, Mommy, you look pretty. Where you going?" Raylynn asked, running in the room.

"Thank you, baby. I'm going out. Where your granny?" Gabriel grabbed her Birkin and picked Remi up.

Raylynn led them out the room and downstairs to where her granny was awaiting them. The girls were leaving, and the boys were at Stprix's, so she was about to be kid free.

"Hey, Pooh! You look good, yo' husband about to let you go out like that?"

"Bye, Momma. Thanks for watching them." She kissed her mother, Yolanda's, cheek while passing Remi off.

Ray walked in the foyer where they were standing. He took one look at Gabriel and mugged her, and Yolanda nor Gabriel missed it. Yolanda laughed while he hugged and kissed both of his daughters goodbye.

"You need some money?" Ray asked his mother-in-law.

"Nope but I want some." She held her hand out. He stuck his hands in his pocket, pulled out a huge stack of bills, and handed it to her.

"Thank you, son. We about to get out of here so you can handle your business," Yolanda teased, and Gabriel smacked her lips.

She hugged and kissed her children goodbye, and Yolanda walked out with them. Ray locked the door.

"Why are you locking the door when you know I'm about to leave?" Gabriel folded her arms across her chest as he angrily peered at her.

"If you tryna go out, I suggest you go change. Or stay in the house… the decision is yours to make."

"Ray, I'm not going to change. What's wrong with what I'm wearing?" She raised her voice and he stepped toward her, getting in her face.

"You must want a nigga to die tonight. Yo' whole ass hanging out. Shid, I don't know why you even just came down here looking like that." His frown deepened, letting her know just how angry he was.

"Cause I'm grown as fuck." She matched his anger.

"Okay, you so grown gon' and leave. I'ma come embarrass the fuck out of you. You think I want my wife ass out at the club for other niggas to see?"

"That bitch you fucked or fucking be having her whole body out in the strip club for the whole world to see and you don't say shit," she said, purposely trying to get under his skin.

"I don't give a damn about that bitch. You listening to a bitch that ain't seen my dick since we got married."

"What about before, huh, Ray? You think I care that we wasn't married, cheating is still cheating!" She raised her voice, getting frustrated with him.

"Baby, I swea on my daughters, I had sex with that girl twice. After you found out about it, I never even looked her way again," he explained himself even though back then, they technically weren't together.

She believed him. He didn't give her reasons to doubt him. Back then, she had cut him slack because he was mourning. However, he

GLITZ

had gotten all the grace he was gon' get from her when it came to cheating.

"So, why that bitch in my DMs?" Gabriel asked, putting her hand on her hip. He couldn't help but to admire her beautiful body. He loved his wife and wouldn't do anything to jeopardize their union.

"I saw her last night at the club and when she tried to come in the section, I told her no but I told her homegirl she could come. She was trying to argue with ol' girl and I told her to take her hating ass on. That's the truth, baby. I swear on your life. Why would I fuck up what we got? I ain't stupid." After experiencing Gabriel, he knew he loved her more than he loved Vivian. He missed her daily but if she had not of died, he wouldn't have met his soulmate. He stepped towards her, and she stepped back. He wrapped an arm around her waist and rubbed in between her legs with his free hand.

"I hate you." She moaned as he rubbed her flower in a circular motion.

"No you don't. I would never cheat on you. I promise, okay? I already lost one wife, you think I would be foolish enough to lose you over some dumb shit." He eased his hand inside her thong, connecting their flesh that loved to be up against each other.

"Okayyy." She moaned even louder than before.

"You love me?" He stared into her eyes while he stroked her center.

"Yesss!"

"I love you too, baby. Can I eat my pussy?" He asked, speeding up his strokes. She wrapped her arms around his neck and held him tightly as her body twitched.

"Yes." She kissed his lips, and he eased his tongue in her mouth. He pulled his hand out her panties and picked her up.

"I'm sorry," she apologized as he carried her onto the elevator. She had been being mean to him all day long.

"I don't need an apology. I just want you to trust me. "

"Ray you know I trust you." She argued as he stepped off the elevator. He carried her to their bedroom and dropped her on the bed.

"I can't tell." He removed his clothes while she did the same.

"You're right. Let me make it up to you." She pulled him in the bed with her and took his soul over and over again until he was drained and completely speechless.

* * *

Signy, Nya, and Jocelyn were out having a girls day out.

"So, Jocelyn? How long you staying this time?" Nya asked.

"A week. I miss my god kids," she replied in reference to Signy's three children.

Story was six about to be seven, Sabella was five, and Sahana was four. Signy had all girls, and she wasn't mad about it. After all, she had seven boys that she loved just like she birthed them.

"Hoe, you didn't miss me?" Signy rolled her eyes.

"I talk to you every day, best. I do miss you, though, sometimes not gonna lie."

"You miss me all the time. You and Quin might as well move here to be with us. That way y'all can get y'all's kids any time y'all want."

"We've been thinking about it. Well not moving-moving but getting a house here so we can spend summers and stuff with them."

"Ouuu, please!" Signy dropped her fork and held her hands together like she was praying.

"I thought me and Kay were bad, y'all hoes pitiful." Nya laughed.

"That's her, you know she used to lick pussy. I think she thinks she's my girlfriend. I done told you." Jocelyn playfully pointed her finger in Signy's face.

"And I done told you I don't want yo' ass." Signy smacked her hand away, causing Jocelyn to laugh.

Signy was thankful for her best friend and her children's mothers. They had all become friends after all they were family. They finished eating then left. Signy and Jocelyn were together as they cruised to Signy and Stprix's home.

Signy pulled into the garage. They got out and walked inside. They cracked up, laughing at the sight of all the girls at the door awaiting their arrival.

Signy hugged and kissed them and then Jocelyn did the same.

"Mommy, come on so you can look what I made for you and my Gommy today at school." Story grabbed Signy's hand and led everyone to the kitchen where her paintings were plastered on the refrigerator.

She took them down and passed them both one.

"Awww, Gommy loves it! Thank you, baby." Jocelyn hugged her again while placing a kiss on top of her head.

"Me too it's so pretty. Thank you, Stank." Signy smiled at her sweet and thoughtful child. They heard the garage come up again, and the girls looked in the direction of the garage.

"Daddy!" Story shouted as she took off with her sisters right behind her.

A few minutes later, Stprix walked in with Story on his back and Sabella in one hand and Sahana in the other. His girls were daddy's girls through and through.

"You going out with us, tonight?" Signy asked Jocelyn.

"I don't really feel like it. Do y'all mind if the girls stay with me?"

"Yes!" Sabella exclaimed, throwing her arms up in the air.

"It's cool with me. Y'all wanna go stay with y'all's Gommy?" Stprix asked, and the girls all said yes in unison.

"Well, come on. Y'all have fun for me." Jocelyn headed for the front door where the Audi she always drove when she was in town was parked. Stprix carried the girls outside to the truck, and then watched as they pulled off, headed toward the guest house that was strictly for Jocelyn and Marquin when they came to town.

* * *

SIGNY WAS out at the strip club with Stox, Storm, and Stprix. Her and Stox were standing on the couch, making it thunderstorm. They were throwing stacks at a time while Storm and Stprix got lap dances. There was ten dancers entertaining them.

"Ouuu, you in trouble." Signy leaned in so that Stox could hear her. He followed her line of vision and looked spooked at the sight of Taliyah, Sagari's mother.

She stormed in their direction and bypassed Stprix's many shooters because they knew her. She jumped up on the couch and started hitting Stox. One of Stprix's men grabbed her, angering Stox.

"Nigga, get your hands off her!" Stox snapped. Stprix jumped up. He knew if he didn't deescalate the situation, Stox would take matters into his own hands. The man let her go when Stprix walked over.

"Y'all lil' crazy muthafuckas chill out," Stprix demanded, looking between his son and granddaughter's mother.

"I'm sick of him. All you do is lie and cheat!" Taliyah folded her arms across her chest. Signy looked around the club and all eyes were on them.

"Come on, let's go," Signy ordered, and they all prepared to make their exit.

"How you get here, Taliyah?" Signy asked her.

"My friend outside."

"Okay you can ride with me, and Stprix you ride with Stox so we can talk," Signy called out as they stood outside the club.

"Ma, I can take her home," Stox said with anger still dancing in his eyes.

"What did I say?" Signy snapped at him, and he smacked his lips but he knew not to utter a word.

Taliyah mushed him in the face before following Signy. They got in the car together, and Signy pulled off.

"Why you always insist on embarrassing yourself for a nigga?" She saw a lot of herself in Taliyah and wanted to guide her in the right direction. Taliyah shrugged.

"He makes me so mad. Ever since he got this new status, it's going to his head. Another girl called my phone tonight, and I didn't think I just reacted. Then, I'm pregnant again."

Signy glanced in her direction while getting on the interstate. Taliyah had been in their lives for a minute.

"If you're not going to do nothing about him cheating or leave, then let that man cheat in peace."

"Ma, how can you say that?" Taliyah looked at her like she was hurt.

183

GLITZ

"Because you need to hear the shit. Don't you get tired of acting like this every other day? Leave his ass and watch him get his shit together. I know you love him but love yourself more. He's not going to stop cheating until you make him value you but all this rah-rah shit every time we turn around is crazy. I know you're tired. Then, you're pregnant that's not good for the baby."

"I know." Taliyah sighed. She did love Stox. She loved him a lot. He was her savior and the love of her young life. It would hurt for her to leave him but she knew it needed to be done. They arrived at Stprix and Signy's house, one right after the other.

"Where's Gari?"

"At my house with my sister."

"I'll be to get her tomorrow," Signy let her know as Stox stood at the passenger door. He already knew why she had whooped his ass. He told himself he was going to avoid her and let her calm down and plead his case at a later time. However, his plan backfired in the worst way.

"Okay. How I'ma get home? I don't want to deal with him tonight," she spoke to Signy while staring at him.

"You can drive my car. I wasn't trying to hurt your feelings but sometimes, we need some tough love. Boss up on that nigga. I love you. Be careful.

"I am, I promise. Thank you, I love you too," Taliyah said as Signy unlocked her door. She got out, and Taliyah climbed in the driver seat. Stox ran around to the driver side and pulled on the door handle.

Taliyah peeled off, almost running his toes over in the process.

"Why you let her leave?" Stox questioned Signy while Storm and Stprix looked on in amusement.

"I told her to leave yo' ass and not just for tonight. I told her to leave you and see how you like it. I bet yo' ass will stop cheating, then won't you? You think that shit cute?" Signy raised her voice, and he dropped his head.

Stprix unlocked the door, and him and Storm walked inside to give them privacy.

"Mama," Stox said lowly. He had two mothers that didn't mind going in his shit when he was wrong.

"Don't fucking mama me, Stox Alexander! You're wrong, baby. I love you, Lord knows I do, but I'm going to tell you when you ain't right. You better stop treating that girl like that, you gon' be sick if another nigga snatch her up and treat her like she should be treated —"

He went to open his mouth but she shot him a stern look.

"You mad 'cause I'm saying it, imagine if it happens. I know you're young and you have this new status but don't walk all over the one person that loves you and loved you before you got that status. If you want to date other people, you need to let her go and stop dragging her along and having her thinking you're going to be faithful to her. How would you feel if some lil' nigga walked all over and played with Sagari, Story, Kenya, Sabella, or Hana's emotions? On top of that, Taliyah is the mother of your children."

"I know, Ma. I'ma get my shit together I swea."

"Whatever, Stox. I'll believe it when I see it. Bring yo' ass in this house you not going over there to harass that girl," Signy warned. He laughed because she knew him well. She knew exactly what was on his agenda.

He followed Signy inside and locked the door behind him. The smell of food had them walking towards the kitchen. Chef had prepared them a late night meal per Storm's request. Him and Stprix were at the table eating. Signy and Stox washed their hands. Signy fixed their plates then they joined Storm and Stprix.

"Ma must've made you come in," Storm cracked, causing Stprix to laugh.

"Storm, don't make me get on you 'cause you ain't no better."

"Ma- ma this ain't got nothing to do with me. My girl didn't walk up in no club and Floyd Mayweather me." Storm continued to cut up. Everyone laughed except Stox, who took his plate and left the kitchen.

"Baby, come back! Y'all so childish," Signy fussed at Storm and Stprix, who were still laughing.

GLITZ

"Shid you was laughing too," Stprix defended, and Signy rolled her eyes at him.

Storm was next to go. He put his plate in the sink and kissed Signy's cheek before slapping hands with Stprix. Stprix's oldest two children had become his best friends. The three of them were joined at the hip along with Fox and Jaquie. Once Stprix and Signy were done eating, they headed upstairs to their room and got ready for bed.

"Don't be telling that girl to leave him, you know he ain't playing with a full deck."

"Yeah like somebody else I know," she mumbled but he heard her. He smacked her ass hard as he followed her out the bathroom to their bed. They climbed in and cuddled up close together.

"You remember when I left you for a whole year and how that made you feel?"

"Hell yeah that was the saddest most depressing year of my life. I ain't just saying that. I was sick as fuck without you," he admitted.

"I know and that's what his ass needs," she said while Stprix rubbed her ass.

"Thank you for taking me back. I don't know where I would be without you, baby girl. I love you, Fat."

"We locked in, twin. I love you more. You've been perfect. You're the best husband and father in the world. There's no other place I'd rather be than with you and all ten of my kids."

"Eleven," Stprix corrected.

"I know, baby, but she's not here."

"She is in spirit."

"I believe that."

Signy wholeheartedly believed that Saint had been with them and rooting for them every step of the way. After all, her death brought them together and made them fall in love. Signy wished she could reverse the hands of time but she knew everything happened for a reason. Six years later, and her life was just a beautiful as ever.

The End!

Made in United States
Orlando, FL
31 March 2025